Nicholas E Watkins

Hack

1

Hack

Also by Nicholas E Watkins

Tanker

Bank

Dealer

Oligarch

Steel

About the Author

Nicholas Watkins lives on the Coast with his wife and has four children He is a retired Accountant and has a Degree in Economics. He worked in the City of London for many years.

Hack

Chapter 1

It was remote. It was late. It was raining. Not the sort of night many people would venture out if they did not need to do so. He needed to. His need was great and the monster within him demanded it. He fought it but in the end, it always won. He could delay it. He could try and distract it, but in the end it would not be denied.

This was neither the first time nor the second or third. It had been years since he had succumbed. It was always there, waiting, arousing, driving and veracious. It was like a worm that burrowed deep in his brain. It fuelled his desire, while eating his soul.

He stood looking down at her naked body. The neon light, casting no shadows, gave the illusion on an alabaster life sized doll lying unmoving on the bed. He began to undress. His hand shook with anticipation making it difficult to manage his buttons. He breathed deeply in an attempt to control himself. Calmer, more slowly he savoured the moment as he stripped naked. He felt good, powerful, in control.

Now the preparations could begin. From his bag, the bag he always had packed and ready, he removed the hair clippers. They were fully charged he had made sure of that. He had lived this moment a thousand times in his imagination. Over and over in his head, every detail would be envisaged. He would lie in bed, night after night, slowly masturbating as he conjured up the scene that was now a reality.

As he lay in bed he would focus on every detail as he stroked his penis. He had to have it completely right. The nipples, her feet, her toe nails, her hair, he labia they had to be just so in his masturbatory fantasy, He would rerun and rerun it in his mind until the scenario was perfected .He would become more frenzied in his wanking, faster and rougher until he finally ejaculated.

Hands still trembling he switched on the hair trimmers. He began with the pubic hair. She only had a small triangle above the labia but it was wrong. It did not fit the masturbatory ideal he had established in his mind. He was meticulous. Every last hair was removed. He was careful not to scratch or cut the flesh as he trimmed the hair away. He parted her legs and checked that all the hair had been removed from around her anus as well as the labia. She had dark brown hair, all wrong. He needed to ensure every last hair was gone.

He checked her armpits, all clear. Now he set about the hair on her head. He had lived this moment countless times in his mind. He knew that the hair trimmers would clog and that he needed to cut the hair first before using them. He took the scissors from his bag. They had been purchased as a set of hairdresser's scissors on the internet. He began to cut the hair. He carefully gathered up her hair as he cut and placed it in a plastic shopping bag. He would burn it later. He had already bagged her clothes ready for incineration.

He was intelligent enough to know how and why he was where he was. It was not his Mother's fault. She had been abused and sought solace in alcohol and drugs. The pattern of her life was set and followed a well trodden path, drugs, prostitution and more of the same.

She had cleaned up her life enough for Social Services to let him be returned to his Mother from the foster careers he had been with on and off since he was born. It did not last. She was vulnerable, lacking in education and self-esteem. It was only a matter of time before she was hooked on drugs and being pimped.

By the time he was ten years of age his mother had completely lost control. They lived in squalor, moving frequently. He had to fend for himself. The flat was a mess of empty beer cans, tin foil and accumulated rubbish. There were visits by Social Services. Overworked and understaffed, they had no real appetite to deal with the situation. His mother usually high or drunk would refuse access or make excuses. They did not follow up.

As his mother's mental condition declined and she became more detached from reality she became less and less engaged with him. He was a burden to her. She no longer cared about anything other than where her next hit of crystal or crack was coming from. She sold everything she had for drink and drugs. She sold the furniture, his toys, her body and then his body.

First she would make him join in as she entertained, but she found that selling him brought bigger money than she could earn with her drug ravaged body. The pimps were soon on the case. He was a money tree for them and his mother.

She was too far gone to really understand what she was doing. He took the abuse and changed inside. He hated. The hatred, pain and humiliation mutated. His translated his natural love for his mother into a desire to hurt her, to abuse her. He had watched his mother time and time again, smoke or inject some drug or other. He had watched her fuck, suck countless men. He wanted some of the love the men were getting. It was an Oedipus complex with a desire to kill.

His mind had rejected the worst of it all. The memories that lingered were of her painted toe nails and her long hair. He had found her overdosed and naked. She had died while whoring. The punter had fled, but not before finishing what he had paid for. He had watched her naked, still. He was twelve. He touched her and enjoyed the feel. He masturbated.

His life changed. He was adopted. He was sent to private school. He went to University and it turned out he had a brilliant

7

mathematical brain. He could forget all in the beautiful patterns that mathematics wove in his mind. It was purity. It was clean. It was unlike his life.

Then came the humiliation, a woman, woman with the look and feel of his mother had raised the demon. The feelings deeply repressed, held in check for years, were uncorked. The woman naked before was not that woman, but for now she would do until he could get her.

He did not rush. He took his time, adding to the anticipation and his arousal. Having cut the hair short enough, he finally he began to shave her head. His hands trembled as he shaved her head. Finally he finished and put the scissors and trimmer back into his bag.

He reached out and slowly fondled her breasts and felt his penis become even firmer in his arousal. They were soft. He bent his head to her chest and sucked her nipples, first one then the other. He wanted them erect. The blood was drawn into them and as they filled they enlarged. The areola went from pink to a dark purple as his sucking caused the bruising.

He stroked his penis, heightening his arousal. He parted her thighs so he could get a better view of her vagina. Riga mortis had not set in. He had time before the onset. She was still pliable. She was still available.

He walked across the cold and bare concrete floor to the steel work bench. He was aware of the rain outside as it clattered on the galvanised roof covering the disused engineering work shop. The small complex of industrial units was set well back from the road on a farm. There were four in total. They were in a single storey, long, grey, concrete building. Electricity and water had been laid. The other three units were vacant. The old industries had died and they were not suitable to the more modern requirement of the tech age.

Next to the pile of tools on the rusty bench sat the polystyrene head. It was featureless with no face, eyes or mouth. The wig sat on it. The hair was long and cut with a fringe to the front. It was perfect, the right colour, the right style. It was exactly as he remembered it. He lifted the wig. It felt right. It was real hair, not something you picked up in a fancy dress shop or a cheap sex shop for role play. It was densely woven, quality. He had it made to his exact specification.

He stood still stroking the hair in his hand. He remembered. Feelings of lust, disgust, and shame all came, flooding his brain with images. Then the feelings of hate came, burning deep, enraging and arousing, in the same instant. His penis was demanding release. He felt it hard in his hand. He was ready.

He walked to the young woman. She was so beautiful, small breasts now with dark circles around her nipples caused by the lividity brought on by his sucking. He stroked her face gently as he lifted her head. He carefully placed the wig on her shaved head. He took his time, despite his intense sexual arousal. It had to be perfect.

One final touch was needed to achieve perfection, to achieve his vision, to obtain the revenge he craved. He went back to the bench and picked up the nail vanish, a perfect ruby red. He lifted her foot and inserted the toe separator. Carefully he began to paint. Painstakingly he applied the vanish, ensuring that it did not bleed onto the toes themselves. The smell of pear drops filled the air as he applied a second coat. He waited, watching her naked body, slowly masturbating, as he waited for the varnish to dry.

He could wait no longer. The rage and hatred seized him. Now she would pay, pay for the humiliation, the feeling of impotence. He felt the power in him. He felt the strength. Now was the time, his time to take back his life, to feel the strength of the man he was. He punched, beat and did as he wanted. Now he was in control.

He sat covered in perspiration surveying the beaten and broken body of the young girl. He was trembling. His mouth hung open

9

and his eyes glazed as he waited to come down from the high, the euphoria. It had been nearly eighteen months since his last kill. He knew that he could not wait that long again. He knew the desire was getting stronger. He thought he had gained control, but that bitch had set it all off again.

She had humiliated him. She had made him look a fool. She had brought it all back. She had tricked him. Not the mutilated girl before him. She had only been a substitute. A stand in to relieve the demands of his penis, an interlude, or perhaps the prelude to getting his ultimate satisfaction.

The first time he had killed, he had not planned it. She was a prostitute. He was in a foreign land. He had not planned it. He was drawn to her. She was the right type. He had not meant to kill but he was driven to it. He had tried to fuck her, but he could not get an erection. He was angry and started to strangle her. As the breath left her and she began to go limp, he felt the power rise within him.

He left the Country the next day. Now back in England, he had planned it and was more thorough. He took the wig from the body and replaced it on its stand. He carried the body to the old bath he had bought a month previously. It was filled with bleach. She would soak, removing all traces of DNA.

He would return and take the body from the bath in twenty four hours. She would be wrapped in a plastic sheet and placed in the chest freezer. He would use the electric saw to cut the body into more manageable sized pieces to store. He knew that rigor mortis would set in, but should pass after a few days making the body flexible again and easier to butcher.

He knew that he could not keep an indefinite number of bodies in and infinite number of freezers. He knew he had to work out a way of disposing of them. By freezing and bleaching he knew that it would be hard for any forensic pathologist to say, with any certainty, the time or place of death. He also hoped that with no body for a prolonged period, the investigation would be that of a missing person rather than a murder.

He took the bags of clothing and hair and put the burner to the rear of the units. He watched and made sure all was reduced to ashes. He was left with some non-combustibles, some jewellery, a clasp and chain from her hand bag, metal buttons, nipple ring and belly bar. He would place them in different rubbish bins over the next few weeks.

As he drove away, he started to plan on how he would acquire his next victim. He knew that the next would only be another substitute to keep his beast at bay until he could truly take his revenge on the bitch who had humiliated him. That would take time, but he would get her and in the meantime the anticipation of using her was so delicious.

Chapter 2

Panos stood on the castle ramparts looking down on the river Danube as it flowed between Buda and Pest. He was amazed how much it had changed since the last time he had been here. It had been almost twenty two years since he had been here. Things had certainly changed, not only for Hungary but for him.

Then he had been riding high, a senior position within the bank he worked for, he had come to Budapest to oversee the integration of the computer systems at the newly opened branch. The place then was a mix of the old communist guard, with Russian connections still pulling the levers of power and the new western businesses eager to rekindle the economy. The Germans and Austrians led the charge. The business that had flourished with the ties established over the centuries as part of the old Austro-Hungarian we back. The first in had been the German insurance companies then the banks.

The rule of communism had left the Capital a grubby, uncared for mess. The grand buildings of Budapest were dirty, scarred and neglected. He remembered going to the opera house. The building was black with grime from the poorly produced cars that emitted a continuous stream of soot from their exhausts. The whole centre of the city was in the same grubby state. The inside had, however, been maintained, after all the Communist great and good held meetings there.

Panos had arrived early that day and had a walk round the centre. It was an amazing transformation. The buildings were clean, the opera house restored to its former glory. The major retailers had arrived and all the brands had jumped on board. The shopping area had been pedestrianised and was now packed with tourists and locals. The seedy bars, run by the so-called Russian Mafia, had been cleaned out and the dodgy street money changers had now ceased to exist when Hungary adopted the euro. Of course, the porn and drugs were still there, as in any major conurbation, but were now banished to the back streets.

As he looked down at the boats and cruise ships moving under the bridge below him, Panos could see that Budapest's regeneration over the last twenty five years contrasted starkly with the decline in his own fortunes. He had left the Bank and at first had gone freelance, then a small business then a big business. Ten years ago he was riding high and ready to retire and move back to Cyprus.

He had been ten when the Turks had invaded Cyprus, in July nineteen-seventy-four. His family's land, home and everything they owned had been taken or destroyed by the invaders. A Greek military junta had orchestrated the overthrow of the Cypriot Government and installed a new puppet president. The Turks responded by invading. The Koumis had to run. He remembered the panic and the fear. They had been forced to leave his grandmother who was too frail to travel. Panos never got to see his grandmother again. There were reports of atrocities committed by both sides. The Turkish Army and the Greek side both conducted ethnic cleansing in the areas that came under their control. His father had been captured by the Turks and so Panos and his elder brother and arrived in England penniless and homeless. His father had finally been released and had joined them. He was broken and his health was poor. He died within two years.

The Koumis made their way in England and by two thousand and eight Panos was ready and had the funds to move back to Cyprus and buy a small piece of his heritage back. Then the financial crash came and he was bankrupt before he knew it. He had turned all his assets into cash, bought a large plot of land in Cyprus, not far from the village where his wife had lived as a child. He had moved his money to the Cypriot Bank and authorised the transfer to the contractor to build the dream villa for him and his wife.

He had mortgaged their home in London to the maximum. The property market was riding high. He had bought the land in Cyprus and sold his business. He had the funds and set about sorting the building of their home on the Island. Panos put his money in the bank in Cyprus, but the Island's Banking sector was little more than a front for offshore tax evasion and its business model was based on the billions of illicit Russian Oligarch money. The Country's economy collapsed and it had to take EU and IMF funding to survive. Then the Bank of Cyprus, heading for collapse, made a grab for the depositor's money.

The contractor who he had paid to build their dream villa collapsed overnight. His house was repossessed in England, leaving him in debt to the tune of over four hundred thousand pounds. The value of the land he had bought to build on in Cyprus plummeted. He was penniless.

As he walked down the hill back to the bridge, he thought of the irony of his situation. He had fled Cyprus without a pot to piss in and he was now back after what seemed a lifetime of living in a cheap flat without a pot to piss in. Then a month ago, a man came knocking and he found himself sitting in the local Taverna.

"Mr Koumi I know this may seem a little unusual," he began. Panos had travelled enough to immediately recognise the man's ethnicity. His accent alone was enough to identify him as Romanian and his appearance confirmed it, dark eyes, black hair that was not that dissimilar to Panos's appearance. The man, who, Panos would later discover was called Andrew Boerescu, was shorter, younger and thicker set than Panos however.

"Would you please say what you want? Your message refers to a job, a project. It is very unspecific."

Boerescue took a sip of the cheap grappa before continuing. He

14

was trying to size up the type of person the man sat in front of him was. He needed to be sure he had judged the situation. Once said, the next few words could not be retracted and then difficulties would flow from the situation, difficulties that would be difficult to solve without violence and the death of his newly met companion.

"I believe that you are currently experiencing a certain level of financial pressure?"

Panos felt offended by the plain statement of fact, it injured his pride. He didn't want to appear desperate, which he was. Boerescue saw his hesitation, but chose to say nothing and wait for the reply. "Things are not going as well as they might," Panos finally replied.

"I work for a group of people who are trying to put a highly qualified and highly motivated team together. They have researched you and your background in computing, and in particular banking and cyber security, makes you an obvious choice to lead such a group." He stopped speaking and studying Panos waited for the reaction.

Panos was highly sceptical of the statements being made. True, his skill set matched. He had written front end packages for all the major banks and was fully aware of the ins and outs of all forms of cyber security, both defence and attack. He was also fully aware, that having sold his company; he was under a very strict clause that was part of the sale agreement, to not compete against his former business. He also knew that, in his mid-fifties, he was not particularly desirable to any potential employer.

"Is this legal?"

"It is from you potential employers point of view."

Panos reflected on the reply. Its meaning was clear. It was a state sponsored operation. Legal to the Country making a cyber attack, but very not legal to the enterprise or country that was the victim. "I see," he said.

There was further silence. Boerescue just sat unmoving as Panos took a sip of the cheap brandy, "and?"

"And, how much?"

"One hundred thousand."

"Pounds?"

"Dollars."

"Pounds," repeated Panos.

Panos was now driving to Debrechen, the second largest city in Hungary, about two hours from the capital and close to the Romanian border. The meeting was scheduled for that evening at the Piedmont Hotel. Debrechen was famous as a spa town with its healing thermal springs. He feared that it would be less than relaxing, despite the baths.

He was committed. There was no way back. The closer he came to his destination the more he feared his decision. He needed the money. He was out of options and desperate. "God help me," he whispered as he pulled into the Hotel Car park.

Chapter 3

Madeleine Wilson took a deep breath and walked through the entrance of Thames House. It was her first day at MI5 and she felt the nerves as she made her way through security and was shown to the lift. She sat waiting outside Anthony Burr's office, the head of the organisation. She was to be the new deputy Director.

She was fifty three years of age and slightly overweight. She was of Afro-Caribbean descent and had started her life as a police woman. Her hair was cropped short and she had the appearance of a person who stood for no nonsense. Her years in the police had equipped her to deal with most situations in an orderly, efficient way.

Her career rise had been steady and organised. From the beat to the higher ranks she had progressed solidly. Her cool head and analytic personality made her the ideal candidate to appoint to the Police National Counter Terrorism Unit. She, until recently, had been deputy head at their headquarters, with overall responsibility for planning and strategy and for providing support services to the Police Counter Terrorism Network for England and Wales. The other key area of NCPHQ was to provide a coordinated counter terrorism approach in partnership with the other agencies, the government, MI5 and other special braches of the police and agencies.

She was aware that MI5 was under scrutiny. There had been a spate of terrorist attacks up and down the Country. This type of attack was becoming the norm, a single individual acting alone, claming allegiance to the Islamic State, the extremist Muslim organisation that would attack and kill. The attacks often were unsophisticated. The killer would mow pedestrians down using a car or truck, or use a machete or big knife to attack unsuspected diners outside a restaurant. The lack of sophistication nevertheless did not reduce their devastating impact.

Some of the attackers had been on the radar of MI5 and questions were being asked to its effectiveness. Its practices, its approach and its governance were all under scrutiny. There were calls for a Public Enquiry. Politicians were calling for more funding. Madeleine knew she was moving into the hot seat and she relished the challenge.

The vacancy had come available with the previous deputy, Harry Denham's, sudden retirement. There were rumours that there had been some sort of major bust up with Anthony Burr. The details were unclear, but one thing was clear, the head of the Met, Christopher Moon, had fallen out big time with MI5 over the affair. In part Madeleine's appointment was an attempt to get matters back on an even keel. The hope was that as a copper she would be able to paper the cracks between MI5 and the UK's biggest police force.

The main problem facing the Agency was that, even if it knew of all the potential threats currently in progress, monitoring them was not a simple task. One individual of interest was capable of draining resources at an alarming rate. Full time surveillance required upwards of twelve agents per suspect. Then that expanded exponentially as the suspect's associates became known and tracked. Add to that electronic surveillance provided around the clock by GCHQ, the governments ears consisting of over five thousand individuals based in a doughnut shaped building outside Cheltenham and the resource required to monitor just one possible threat was enormous. Currently MI5 had over twenty seven thousand persons of interest to monitor.

"Sit down, call me Tim, everyone does" said Anthony Burr.

Madeleine sat opposite the smiling man in his mid-forties. He was in his own way handsome, medium build with a surprisingly gentle personality for a man in charge of such an organisation coping with so much pressure and scrutiny. "I am glad to be here."

"And we are glad to have you here," he said to the young woman, in her mid-twenties, that occupied the seat next to Madeleine on the opposite side of the desk to Tim. "This is Harriet Shaw, head of cyber stuff."

Madeleine acknowledged the young woman and waited for Tim to continue. Instead Harriet spoke. "You have Denham's old office and staff. Here are you access codes etc. for files, computers and restricted parts of the buildings. You will also find details of our other offices and facilities scattered around the Country and field agent details and protocols." She handed her a large bound folder and an envelope with the usual "Top Secret" logo on.

"Well that's that all sorted, tea or coffee?" said Tim.

Tim having acted as mother they sat with their tea or coffee and Tim's favourite Hobnob biscuits in front of them. "So what's new?" Tim usually kept to a daily routine. He started with Cyber and Harriet first. Then the various heads of departments followed on at fifteen minute intervals. Today they were all offset by half an hour to allow Tim to ease Madeleine into her new role.

As head of MI5 Tim's role was more or less oversight and administrative until the there was a biggy and the shit hit the fan and decisions needed to be made. He received updates and briefings routinely to his computer, but he liked the personal touch. He learnt early on, when reading a file it was easy to miss a significant aspect or to fail to grasp the nuances of a situation. By meeting with the players on a routine basis, he knew in few words he would be appraised of the key issues that needed his personal attention.

"We have seen a gradual intensity of hacking on all types of systems coming from Russia, the Ukraine and North Korea. There are a mixture of the state sponsored pain in the arse type fishing for

Hack

weaknesses in MI5, MI6 and the other Government departments and criminals trying to hold businesses to ransom by locking up their computers, then asking them to pay a small fee to restore the files."

"They were quite successful with screwing over the National Health Service computers recently," said. Madeleine.

"Ransom?" said Tim.

"It would seem so, but they ask for bit coins so they can't be traced but don't bother to collect. We can, of course, track bit coins. We hacked it ages ago. The number of people who actually paid the ransom was miniscule, considering the scope of the hack. The total bit coin sterling equivalent was less than nine thousand pounds."

"A lot of work for very little reward," said Tim.

"And what they got, they left untouched," said Harriet.

"What about the North Koreans, they like to mess about and cause as much disruption as they can?" asked Madeleine.

"Unusually quiet for once," said Harriet.

"Well, they have just launched a new intercontinental ballistic missile, probably gives Kim Jong-un something to distract him from hacking," said Tim, "Anything else?"

"Can you guess who my new liaison officer is at GCHQ?" said Harriet.

"James Bond?"

"Almost, Kevin Drew." Drew had been at MI5 working for the now retired Harry Denham. He had been ousted along with his boss when they were discovered working together to discredit Tim in a power grab.

20

Madeline looked puzzled. "I'll tell you all about that later," said Harriet.

Turning to Tim she continued, "He is fine and seems to be letting bygones be bygones. In any event, has done rather well from the move, massive promotion and a big fat pay rise."

"Keep your eye on him. Now let's do some real work," said Tim.

Chapter 4

Panos had spent a comfortable night in the Hotel Divinus in Debrechen. Boerescu arrived mid-morning along with four associates. Although there were a varied mix of nationalities, they, all to his relief, shared a common language, English.

"Let's go outside where we cannot be heard," said Boerescu. They walked through the lobby and into the paved area in front of the hotel. There was a selection of table and chairs. He selected a table out of ear shot of the other guests.

"I am thinking that we should do 'A Reservoir Dogs' and not know each others identities," said Boerescu. He was smiling as he continued, "Who wants to be Mr Pink?"o

They all laughed. "I don't mind, it fits after all." A young blonde man with his hair coiffed replied. His was no more than twenty or twenty-years old. Clearly gay, he walked with an exaggerated swing of the buttocks to ensure that, to anyone observing, his orientation would be apparent.

"This is going better than I thought," continued Boerescu.

Panos became Mr White. A thick set man in his thirties, who Panos realised, was probably Russian or Ukrainian became Mr Black. Mr Red was a short individual, either Chinese or Korean. Finally, Mr Blue was named, a fat jolly American kid of around nineteen.

A waiter arrived with shot glasses and a bottle of schnapps. Boerescu poured the liquor and raised his glass. "To success and wealth," he voiced the toast. He took the glass and drained it in one go, slamming the now empty vessel onto the table.

They followed suit. Mr Blue coughed violently and nearly threw up. He turned a bright shade of red as the schnapps burnt its way down into his stomach. Seeing the colour of his complexion, Boerescu said, "Fuck! Perhaps you should have been Mr Red. No I was right the first time, you are definitely turning blue." Mr Red continued coughing and indeed was turning blue.

Mr Black poured himself another shot. "Not bad, but not as good as Russian," he said downing it in one.

"You should try raki or grappa," said Panos.

"What the fuck is that?" said Black.

"It's made from grapes rather than grain. When I say grapes, I mean the left overs when the juice has been extracted for wine. Skins, stalks, basically any edible plant material. It's fermented and distilled."

"Does it taste good?" asked Pink.

"Well, I wouldn't say that, but it grows on you after a bit," said Panos.

"So does athletes foot," said Red. The Chinese was the least talkative of the group and obviously had no taste for alcohol. It was apparent to all present that humour was not his strong point. He was what would be described as intense, or focussed.

Mr Pink took his second drink and making an exaggerated cocking of his little finger drank it down. It was clear that he was a party animal and was quite happy to go for it. Mr Blue was still looking like he was about to vomit and had turned from red to green.

It was only ten in the morning, but they were all on their way to being pissed. Mr Blue tried to refuse to participate, but when American prestige was put on the line by Mr Black, the Russian throwing down the gauntlet. He re-entered the fray.

The party continued for a further hour. It had been planned this way by Boerescu. There is nothing like a good piss-up followed by a monster hangover to bond a group. This was not the conventional approach to team building adopted by most organisations. Some form of working together was the common method. Finding your way through a forest, fording a river or tacking an obstacle course that relied on interdependence was the norm. The Romanian way, as promulgated by Boerescu, was get them rat-arsed.

Suitably bonded, it was time for the group to depart. Boerescu had organised their check-in and luggage transfer to a waiting executive mini bus. The driver had come to the table and reminded them that it was time to depart. They all got up, with the exception of Mr Blue, the American kid. He was sound asleep. It was still only eleven-thirty in the morning. Mr Black casually pulled the unsteady Blue to his feet. "Fucking Americans, all mouth and no trousers," he said as hoisted him over his shoulder with Boerescu's help and carried him to the waiting transport.

"We have about an hours drive to where you will be working and staying," said Boerescu, as the driver started the engine and they drove off. Pink had the foresight to pick up a bottle of schnapps from the table as they left. The party continued as they drove through the Hungarian countryside.

Debrechen still had the look of communism about it as they left the centre and drove through the suburbs. The unflattering, anonymous grey blocks had been shoddily erected to provide housing. They served their purpose, but that was all that commended the architecture. The rural landscape looked unremarkable, save for the occasional older traditional farm dwellings. Panos could see, that compared to his native Cyprus, the buildings we designed with steeper roofs and wood was a favourite cladding material. The harsher winters accounted for the variance.

They arrived at their destination. It was clear it was off the beaten track, deliberately chosen to remain discreet. The entrance was up a gated track past paddocks, where horses cold be seen grazing. The buildings themselves were modern. They were shown to their rooms all en-suite. There was a kitchen for their use for snacks and drinks.

Having settled in, they assembled in a dining area where a buffet lunch was on offer. There was a variety of food on offer to cater for the differing nationalities. However, being Hungary, meat was the dominant ingredient.

They were all in a merry mood with the exception of Blue. He was awake but still fragile and was clearly not in the mood to party further. This did not however deter the remaining colours from indulging.

"Before we get so pissed we can't remember what the fuck we are here for, I should like you to follow me and have a tour of the facilities," said Boerescu. The group raised themselves from the communal dining table and followed their host from the residential complex across the yard to the barn. There was a paddock to one side containing what Panos surmised to be the prize breeding stallion.

"Well at least he will get a fuck," said Red. "There is a distinct lack of women here."

"I'm available, if you boys get lonely," said Pink.

"No, I'll manage somehow," said Black.

"Do not worry gentlemen. Hungary has some of the best whores in the World. We will party when we have worked,"

The door to the barn had a keypad entry system. Boerescu led them down a corridor and opened the door at its end. They stepped inside. "Fuck me," said Blue. Pink raised an eyebrow, but avoided the provocation to camp it up.

Panos was taken aback. Money had been spent here. The kit was the best. The computers, servers, screen and even the furniture was top of the range. Whoever had put this together was serious.

"Deadly serious," thought Panos. He knew at that point that they had been brought together and brought here to perform a specific task. This was not to be some second rate hack, it was military grade. The investment showed intent. This was not aimed at making a couple of bucks by locking a few files on a company's computer system for ransom. This was state of the art cyber attack territory.

Chapter 5

It was still dark when Soo Mi was woken by the ringing of the fire alarm in the dormitory, where she slept along with eighty other young women. There was no fire. The alarm was used every morning at four thirty to rouse the young women. It would be light at five thirty and dark at around nine. She and the other young women would be in the fields picking tomatoes until the light ran out.

She dragged herself out of bed and joined the queue for the toilets. There were eight toilets and ten hand basins. There were also six showers and the girls were on a rota that saw them have access twice a week. Soo Mi's shower was not due for another two days. Having finally gained access to the toilet, she joined the queue for the hand basins.

Her turn finally came and she washed her face, brushed her teeth and used her flannel to clean her bottom and genitals. She knew she was beginning to smell. The long hours picking tomatoes in the summer heat naturally caused perspiration. She would have liked to have used deodorant, but with the money she got to keep each week it was a luxury she couldn't afford. She consoled herself that it was her shopping day tomorrow. She would be allowed out for three hours and walk to the local village where she would spend her weekly allowance on essentials and a treat, like a bar of chocolate.

The local shop keepers knew that the girls from the tomato farm only had the small window to spend their weekly earnings and took full advantage of their situation. There was one price for the Polish locals, who after all could easily shop elsewhere or on line and

27

another for the girls, who had no option but to pay the inflated prices.

She joined the queue for the breakfast. The clock was ticking and Soo Mi was worried she would not get her food before they were loaded onto the bus and taken to the field to begin their twelve hour shift. Breakfast was porridge and sweet tea. Lunch would be delivered to the fields and usually bread, cheese and cold sausage. A hot evening meal, usually potatoes, vegetables and some type of stew, was served on their return The food was adequate if unsuited to the Korean palate of the girls,

The whistle was blown by the head foreman and the bus was loaded to drop the girls off to start the days picking. The bus only had seating for fifty. They sat three to the two seats that ran the length of the coach or stood as they were driven the three miles to waiting crop.

They passed the sorting and packing plant where another batch of Korean girls was leaving their dormitory to begin their days labour. Soo Mi looked from the window as the tired women traipsed across the yard. The factory was surrounded by high wire fences and access and exit was only possible through the manned security gate. The compound where Soo Mi slept only had the one locked entrance and was surrounded by a high fence. They were not prisoners, but they were discouraged from wandering off.

North Korea was desperate for hard currency. The sanctions imposed on the Country made it very difficult to earn foreign currency. China and Russia conveniently ignored the sanctions, helping to sustain the dictatorship of Kim Jon-un, but the export of cheap labour was a very big contributor to the coffers. In effect, Countries could bid for what amounted to slave labour. The men worked in construction and the women in factories and farms. Poland took the women for their farms and the men worked in the antiquated engineering works that would otherwise be uncompetitive. The Polish workers could move freely in the

European Union and exercised their right to the full by taking jobs in, mostly, Germany and the UK. The Poles worked for the minimum wage in other EU countries while even cheaper labour, imported from Korea, allowed Polish businesses to keep wages low.

The Korean workers were sold to the highest bidder, be that Poland or one of the Gulf States that needed cheap labour to fuel their construction booms. The worker's wages were paid directly to the North Korean Government and the workers, slaves in effect, were given a small weekly allowance. Girls like Soo Mi had no choice. Their family were hostage to the regime back in their home country. If they claimed asylum the parents and siblings would be imprisoned and sent to labour camps or killed. Countries that took advantage of the slave labour were, of course, aiding and abetting in the export of North Korea's human rights violations. Profits of course came first over any political philosophy. Pressure had been brought to bear to stop its member Countries taking part in, what is in effect, modern day slavery supporting one of the World's most evil regimes, but there are always ways round regulations.

Soo Mi started her shift working her way along the rows of tomatoes. They were expected to pick at a set pace. Failing to select and pick the tomatoes at their correct level of ripeness, or failing to pick the right weight would mean she would not get her break or even miss out on the chance to eat. After three hours she needed a toilet break. To save time, a trench had been dug on the side of the field. There was a narrow bench and you sat with your bottom over the edge with the open sewage pit below. In the summer heat the stench of faeces and urine was stifling. She retched as she defecated. There was no privacy. True, a half-hearted attempt at erecting a wind break that would be used on the beach had been made, but it was soon blown down. She was forced to sit fully exposed.

Soo Mi was twenty four and very beautiful and this was in itself a disadvantage. She dreaded the attentions of the Polish men in charge. They knew that she had no options. It was not rape, but they knew that if she were sent back the consequences would be dire for her and her family, she had to keep them happy. The prettier girls were, effectively, on a rota. The men working alongside them in the fields or the factories saw it has perk of the job. She was often forced to have sex three or four times in the evening. She could refuse and she often tried, but the threat of being returned to North Korea was a threat she had to take seriously. She was not sure if the owners of the farms and factories knew what was going on with the sexual abuse. Logically they had no reason to allow it to happen as there was no profit to be gained by their employees being raped. So she doubted that her abusers really had the power to send her home, but she dared not risk it.

Finally her day ended and she got a hot evening meal. She was trying to keep a low profile but Oskar came to seek her out. "Come we are going to a party," he said. He was a big man with missing teeth and a broken nose. He liked to drink and when he drank he liked to fight. Despite his size his passion for drinking Polish Vodka and fighting meant the more successful he was at the former the less successful he was at the latter, which explained the loss of teeth and the facial rearrangement.

Soo Mi drank the vodka, stripped naked and let the three men in Oskar's filthy little apartment take it in turns to bugger her. She lay on her back her feet held by the two men standing naked either side of her fondling her breasts, while the third pumped away at her anus. When he had ejaculated in her bum they rotated and the next took up buggering her. She felt disgust for herself and hatred for the scum who were fucking her.

She did however love her Country and its leader Kim Jon-un. She was devoted to him. He was her true Father and if this is what he demanded of her she would gladly obey. She knew that perhaps she would give so much more to him. She was ready for the call. She was only too happy to serve the "Great One", happy to give her life for him.

Chapter 6

Kevin Drew arrived at Paddington to be confronted with the carnage of the early morning rush hour. He was about five foot ten, pale skinned, red haired and had the obligatory freckles. This was the one thing he would definitely miss about living in London, the transport chaos which had to be tolerated every working day. By the time he battled his way through the milling hoards of passengers and squeezed onto the tube train he felt tired, sticky and grubby.

His move to GCHQ Cheltenham, the ears of the British Government, had not been voluntary. Two months ago he had a promising career at Thames House with MI5. He had backed the wrong horse, in Harry Denham, in a power play. Denham had failed in his bid for Tim Burr's post as head of MI5. Drew had been part of the collateral damage when Denham was forced to take a Knighthood and early retirement.

He was on his way to meet his former boss at MI5, Harriet Shaw. He really held a deep seated hatred for her. She had exposed him in Denham's play for power. She had set him up and made him look a complete fool in the process. He found that hard to swallow and harder to forget. He had no choice at the moment but to take it, but he would get his chance and she would get payback.

As he walked up to Thames House he composed himself. He would be professional. He would show no hint of the smouldering resentment he harboured towards the Head of Cyber security for MI5.

In truth the move to the Doughnut had been a great success. He had arrived at just the right moment in time. Reshuffles, retirements and funding cuts had left a great big hole into which he fitted perfectly. The increase in cyber-attacks by criminals for gain, teenagers doing it for fun, businesses for profit and States for intelligence had all put pressure on all the Government Agencies, including GCHQ to make the networks more secure. The Russian interference in the recent US Presidential Election had highlighted the vulnerability of the institutions of State and there was a rush to plug the holes. The visible aspect of this was a closer working relationship with cyber security companies, liaison with Government Departments, such as the NHS and awareness and education initiatives for business.

These programmes were the visible face of the war on internet hacking. Below the surface, MI5's primary counter intelligence agency along with GCHQ, were becoming proactive. Rather than sitting back and waiting for an attack, they were becoming proactive. Bogus hacking communities had been set up declaring all types of agenda, from animal welfare to the abolition of nuclear threats. In effect they were creating their own cyber threats and inviting likeminded people to join.

MI5, lead by Harriet Shaw, as it turned out was highly successful in engaging with hackers from around the World. Drew had to admire the scope and ability of his nemeses. She seemed to be a natural born hacker. As a by-product of the project, MI5 had been instrumental in providing the Police and Interpol with vital information that had led to the bringing to book of drug rings, paedophile groups, money launderers and dodgy banking practices, among others.

"Good morning, Harriet, It is nice to see you again," lied Drew. He was sat in one of the conference rooms with a coffee when she walked in.

She sat and observed him as he drank. "It is nice to see you again.

You have done very well for yourself, supremo dirty tricks."

He laughed, "That is not my official title. I am in charge of infiltration of the global hacking community. My departure from MI5 turned out well in the end."

"I do hope we can put that behind us, water under the bridge so to speak and get on with things as they are now."

"I wouldn't have it any other way," He replied, however he was thinking, "You fucking smug bitch, I am coming for you and I am going to fuck you over."

"That's good to hear. Now what brings you here?"

"I have something and I can't make sense of it. Naturally, I immediately thought of you and you devious mind."

"Hit me," she said.

"I would love to do that and smash your smug face in," he thought. He said, "Have a read of these and then I will fill in any gaps."

She opened the files and began to read. Finally after about thirty five minutes she spoke. "I don't get it."

"Neither do I. If I am correct, there is a highly sophisticated, highly organised group of hackers that morph seamlessly from one group to another. They seem to be the same bunch of people who seem to expend huge effort into pretending to be someone else. They launch an attack then disappear. They are extremely sophisticated. They cannot be tracked and we have no idea of their location."

"Surely a lot of their activity is ransom related. The usual, fuck up some entities database and then demand payment in bitcoin. The bitcoin system was hacked yonks ago, by virtually every government intelligence service on the Planet. That makes it pretty easy to track the money and find them?"

"They never touch the money."

"What, that makes no sense. Why spend all that time and money and then not profit."

"That is why I am sat here," said Drew. "Who sets up a sophisticated hacking machine for no monetary gain or without some political agenda?"

"Do you have any leads?"

"None, we are getting nowhere. So here I am at MI5."

"Are you sure all the attacks are from one group?"

"Well, we can't be one hundred per cent. The originating location of the hackers seems, on the face of it, to be all over the Globe. On closer inspection there are tell traces in the way it is routed to suggest a strong correlation that it is the same people pretending to be in a different place. The coding of the software also reinforces that assumption. Let's be honest, if you had written a routine to do something, say like pick out a bit of data from a fragmented computer file and you need to do the same thing again in another routine, you don't sit there and write it all over again from scratch. Of course you don't, you just pick up you sub-routine and drop it into the new application."

"So when you examined the coding, from supposedly different hackers, you found bits of code that suggests common authorship?"

"We did and the conclusion is that for some reason, someone wants us to chase out tails looking for a myriad of different groups around the globe when, in fact, it is one highly professional and highly resourced single group."

Harriet looked at the file. "I agree with you, it definitely is one group."

"Well, it is down to MI5 now. You have the boots on the ground, as they say."

Drew left Thames House and made his way to McDonalds on the corner of Trafalgar Square. He ordered the Mac meal with a chocolate milk share. He stood looking out of the window at the traffic jam outside. Their cliental, enjoying the delights American style dining, was global. French, German, Chinese, Indian they all queued for their burgers. The place was full with tourists grabbing a quick bite before exploring the Capital further.

Drew found himself alongside an oriental male. "Did they buy it?" he spoke.

Without looking at his newly appeared dining companion Drew replied, "Hook, line and fucking sinker." The man left immediately and he was left to enjoy the milkshake.

Chapter 7

Tamsin said "goodnight," to her friends and left the bar. She began the walk up Park Street from the centre of Bristol. She had exams the next day and felt she ought to make at least a token effort at revising. They were not important, more of a mid-term test to judge overall progress. She had already stayed too long in the bar and drunk a little too much but she consoled herself in that she was, at least, making a stab at academia.

Reaching the top of Park Street she saw the hooded figure standing in the shadows of the museum entrance. "What the hell," she thought, "something to relax me, why not?"

Tamsin did not recognise the drug dealer. She was in her second year and knew most of the regular suppliers. It was not entirely unusual to see a new face. Quite a few of the students earned a little on the side by selling to their friends and co-students. Living costs were high and loans low so, unless parents helped out, it was hard to get by.

As she approached the dealer she realised he was probably not a student, too old. She hesitated. There was a bigger than usual risk here. The local dealers fiercely defended their turf, stabbings, beatings and shootings were not uncommon between the rival gangs seeking to maintain and expand their trade. The student dealers were tolerated to an extent as they usually only sold to friends and in the main acquired their product from the locals and so, in effect, still contributed indirectly to the gangs overall income. If the gangs thought they were getting too big for their boots, a beating would usually solve the problem.

A completely unknown face was therefore extremely rare. Tamsin knew she should leave it and go to her regular source, but the recklessness brought on by drink caused her to ignore the little voice in her head. She approached the figure concealed in the half light. "Follow me," he turned and crossed to the other side of the road and went down the turning. She followed.

The parking lights flashed on the white Transit van as the dealer operated the remote locking. She was still some distance behind and watched as he opened the rear doors and stepped inside. The door remained open, an invitation to shop. She was not sure; this was not the usual way the deals were done. Normally the dealer would select a spot away from CCTV and pass you the dope on receipt of the payment. A quick exchange and both were on their way.

Her desire for the drugs overcame her hesitancy. She reasoned that the dealer was not local and feared attack by the gang whose territory he was operating on. Given that scenario it was understandable that he was taking extra precautions to avoid being spotted. So she approached the rear of the Transit.

It was her only and last mistake. As she leaned into the van she was grabbed around the throat and pulled from her feet into the interior. It was fast and it was brutal. She tried to scream and she tried to struggle, but the grip was unrelenting. The killer's thumbs pushed into her windpipe crushing it. She felt the pain, she fought for air, but none could get to her lungs. The last thing she saw was the killer's face, covered in a thin sheen of perspiration and the look of pure ecstasy as he watched her turn blue and die.

He sat silent in the back of the van in the faint glow of the panel light. His chest was heaving, taking in deep gasp of air, partly from the exertion, but more from the overwhelming feeling of sexual arousal that flowed through him. He stroked her lifeless body as he sat in the semi darkness. This was only the first part he told himself. He was trembling as he thought of what was still to come.

Finally he judged himself calm enough to drive, exited the rear and walked to the front of the van. He climbed into the driver's seat still trembling. It had gone exactly as he had seen it in his mind's eye. He felt powerful, in charge. It was as though he had control of everything. The World was bending to his will.

Every fine detail was as he had expected it to be. He had driven to this spot only forty five minutes earlier. He had planned the exact route to and from this point. He had plotted his route to avoid every CCTV and every ANPR camera along the way. He had checked the view from the CCTV to and from where he had parked. It was blind to all watchers, the perfect spot to take his victim.

He knew he had controlled the whole series of events. He had selected that girl. He had seen her in his head. He had willed her to leave the bar. It had been pre-ordained that she would follow the route to where he waited. He had compelled her to follow him to his van. She had no choice. He knew that at that point he was all powerful. He was God. She was his sacrifice.

He focussed only the two and half hour drive. He kept to his route of minor roads avoiding the surveillance cameras. He kept his discipline despite his increasing sexual excitement. The anticipation was burning in his brain, his penis erect reminding him of his need for completion.

Finally he arrived at the isolated industrial complex. He took deep breaths and feeling himself calm enough, he stepped from the cab. He opened the rear doors and the small light came on. Tamsin was laying there as he had left her. He fondled her breasts and slid his hand up her skirt and slid her panties to one side. She was shaved. It was as it should be. He fought the urge to rip her clothing from her and take her there and then. He reminded himself that it had to be as he had pre-determined it to be.

She was naked on the bench inside the grubby workshop. He had shaved her head and placed the wig on the body. Apart from that, she was perfect, her body shaved and her toes painted red. He knew that he was getting closer to his ultimate goal. The next would be perfection, there would be no need for the wig.

He was ready. He thrust his penis into her exposed vagina. He was in ecstasy as he fucked. He raised the knife and stabbed into the body each time he pushed his penis in. By the time he ejaculated the body was just a mass or sliced and bloody meat. The image that filled his mind was of his Mother, the whore that had let him be so abused and used just to fill her crack pipe. She was paying now and so would all the other whores who had humiliated him.

He worked again, cleaning the mess and bleaching the body to remove any trace of him. He was now calm and rational and unlike the raging beast that had the blood lust, he cared about being discovered. He cared about not being detected. After all, he was all powerful. Far cleverer than those that would attempt to trap and catch him. The police could be no match for him. Had he not just proved that? After all, that girl had been under his control, had she not? He had just willed her to appear and she had. He needed no further proof as to his power. How could anyone catch him? He was all powerful and they could be no match for him.

His routine was now firmly established. He knew the bins where he would dispose of her clothing and other possessions. The sanitised body, cut up into manageable pieces was placed, wrapped in polystyrene sheeting in the chest freezer awaiting final disposal.

The police received another missing person's report a few days later. They did not rush their enquiries. It was not unusual in their experience for students to go walkabout for a few days. They liked their drugs, they liked their drink and they liked their sex. They assumed that she would reappear having been shacked up with someone for a few days.

Finally, after three days, they started their search. They traced her last known sighting to the bar where she had been drinking with her friends. The CCTV at the bar showed her leaving alone. She was picked up by the Council Buildings CCTV crossing College Green and then at the bottom of Park Street. Then she vanished. The cameras outside the Museum were at the wrong angle to pick her up. They checked all the surrounding surveillance cameras in the area, but she never appeared again. They checked all the traffic cameras at or around that time and tracked down the owners of cars that were photographed entering or leaving. They interviewed all the drivers but nothing was found.

Her killer had set in motion the train of events that would put his ultimate victim in his grasp. She would not just be another random kill. She was his prize and he was already closing in on her. Not long now and he would have her.

Chapter 8

"This is a nice gesture, taking me out for dinner," said Madeleine as they Walked along Shaftsbury Avenue. It was seven o'clock on a Friday evening, she and Tim were finding it hard to make their way along the pavement, crowded with theatregoers and tourists. London was certainly the party capital of the World. All human life was on view, from the weird and wonderful to the beggars and super rich.

The roads were blocked with traffic, the bars with drinkers, the restaurants with diners and the pavements with pedestrians. The drug dealers were plying their trade and the prostitutes had their cards posted in every phone box and amongst the ads for items for sale in every small shop window. The rough sleepers had grabbed their spot in the doorways of office blocks, laying out their sleeping bags and meagre possessions, to claim their territory. They sat, hands held out waiting with a buff piece of cardboard with a crude crayon message outlining their plight in front of them. "Homeless, blind," and so on. "Please help."

Tim could not reply immediately as a tightly knit group of Japanese tourist heading towards them refused to be separated by even a fag paper's width. They moved en-mass as a single, impenetrable unit along the pavement. They followed their guide, who held aloft a brightly coloured golf umbrella, as a precision marching column determined not to break ranks, even if it meant trampling the other pedestrians underfoot. He was forced into the road and Madeline into a doorway to allow them to pass.

Finally reunited he said, "It is partly work, sorry to disappoint, but

I thought I should involve you in meeting a few contacts."

"I was joking. You don't look the sort of person that does socialising."

"To be Honest, I am not the sort of person that does anything. I only go to the dojo once a week to do martial combat because it is a habit I started at Uni and it is now part of my routine. It is in fact my entire routine." He mused to himself. In truth, with the loss of so many people close to him over the past year, he realised that he was shying away from forming any form of relationships or attachments. It did not pay in his line of work to get too close to anyone, the emotional price could be very high if you did.

"How did you know I love Chinese food?" asked Madeleine.

"I didn't pick the restaurant it chose us," said Tim as they headed into China Town.

Madeline was now intrigued. They made their way past the hustle and bustle of the street life, past the predominantly gold and red facades of the shops and restaurants until Tim stopped outside the Flowing Lotus Restaurant. "We're here," he announced as he held the door open for her to enter.

They were immediately attended to on their entry. The waiter approached them and without a word gestured for them to follow. They were led past all the other diners to a door next to the bar that sat to the rear of the restaurant. It was the pre-theatre rush, every table was full and the waiters rushed to fill the orders in double quick time. The place would be empty in another ten or fifteen minutes as the diners would rush to take their seats for whichever performance they had booked.

The door was opened and the waiter gestured them into the back room. In the centre was a circular table for ten. In the centre of the table was a revolving platform which allowed the seated guests to rotate the various platters and position them in front of each diner in turn. Tim sat, Madeleine followed his lead. "The place is bugged," he said matter of factly.

They waited and a man appeared from an ornate screen that obscured one corner. It was a highly decorated affair in the oriental traditions, clouds, bird, trees and figures in the landscape carrying out their daily chores, such as fishing and taking goods to market. It served the purpose of concealing a door that allowed unobserved access to the street and other parts of the restaurant.

"Mr Burr, I am so pleased you could find the time to accept my invitation and honour my humble establishment with your presence," said Zhen Zhou as he extended his hand.

"Let me introduce my new deputy Ms Wilson," Tim began.

"No need, I know who this sleaze ball is. I was a copper for twenty odd years in the Met, don't forget. This is Zhen Zhou, Triad Boss, drug dealer, pimp, murderer and all round very bad person," said Madeleine.

"So nice to renew our acquaintanceship, madam," smiled Zhou. "Tonight however, I am not here in my capacity as criminal mastermind, but as a friend to Mr Burr and MI5. You may not be aware, but Mr Burr did me a great service, a service that I can never repay and so will always remain in his debt. It would be an unbearable loss of face should I in anyway not show honour and respect to him, that I should have to kill myself rather than live with such shame. So rest assured madam, you are her tonight under my protection as an honoured guest."

"How is your daughter?" asked Tim.

"She thrives, she is a joy to me and she is a credit to her family. She is at University and doing well and thanks to you she has a new life."

"I am glad some good came from it all," said Tim.

"As the Chinese proverb says, "Man who walks down middle of road gets knocked down by cars going both ways. Everyone has to choose sides eventually," said Zhou.

"I am not sure what that has to do with anything?" said Tim.

"Neither am I, but it is the only Chinese proverb I know," laughed Zhou.

"Why are we here?" asked Madeleine.

"To eat and meet someone in private. I will leave you now and your fellow dinner companion will join you directly. Please be calm, I assure you, you are in no danger." He left via the door through which Tim and Madeleine had entered.

Moments later a figure appeared from behind the screen. "Good evening," said Henry Young, His name had been Anglicized for convenience but he was thoroughly Chinese in ethnicity. He was a small man and moved with small jerky movements. He reminded Tim of a sparrow. He seemed to be constantly alert and his eyes were constantly moving and his movements gave the appearance of a man in a state of agitation.

Madeleine sensed the tension in Tim. She instinctively knew that he was wary of the small Chinaman that had just entered their presence. This was a dangerous individual, her years as a policewoman set off warning bells in her head. He walked across the room and seated himself at the table. She looked to Tim for an explanation.

"Meet Henry Young, he is an attaché with the Chinese Embassy in London. Mr Young, please meet Ms Madeleine Wilson, my new second in command."

Young extended his hand across the table and Madeleine shook it. "Pleased to meet the famous police counter terrorist officer. How are you enjoying the move to MI5?"

"Madeleine looked confused at this man's knowledge of her and her job."

Tim was being the usual Tim and letting it all wash over his head. Nothing strange here, dinner in a restaurant run by a gangster and a guest that seem to have the inside track on what you had for breakfast and knew your entire life history. She looked at him and held his gaze questioningly.

"Oh," said Tim realising that Madeleine was possibly looking for a fuller explanation at the recent turn of events. "When I say attaché, I actually mean Chinese spy in Chief in the UK, provocateur, industrial and commercial saboteur, all round fucking pain in the arse."

"A bit harsh, don't forget, without us spies you would be out of a job. You should thank me," said Young.

"I'd rather fucking shoot you," said Tim.

"Not today, today we must put our heads together. We have a problem and it is a big one," said Young as he poured wine into the glasses in front of them.

Chapter 9

Panos and the team had been working hard squirreling away in their computer control centre in Debrechen. The colours of the rainbow names had been abandoned within the first two days and they were now on first name terms, Mr Pink, Justin, Mr Black Vince, Mr Red, Lee and Mr Blue was Chuck. They had found difficulty in remembering their own colours, let alone their work mates. So they just introduced themselves.

Boerescu turned up and the team, in a bid to convince him that anonymity was being maintained, they addressed each other as colours. They were just saying the first colour that entered their heads. It was clear after ten minutes that Boerescu could not remember the assigned colours either and so the colours selected became increasing silly. Panos became chartreuse at one point and Vince Mr Lime Green. Eventually Boerescu worked out what was going on and with ill grace told them to, "stop fucking about."

He gathered the group and began to speak. "We are ready to go to the next phase, an all out attack on the following. The aim is to cause the total collapse in the systems of the following: GCHQ, MI5, MI6, the Counter Terrorist Group and the Police National Database. You have all established a route into the various interlinked systems and we have the malware written and ready to go and bring them down."

"I don't get it," Vince was the first to raise the obvious query. "What's the point? The software you had us develop will just bring their systems down and at best, it will only do that for a matter of hours but most likely minutes, given the combined level of expertise we are facing."

Justin joined in, "There is no money in it either. The hack is not designed to hold them to ransom, it just fucks any system. How do we make money out of that?"

Boerescu demonstrated his true character at that point, thug and enforcer. "We are not having a debate. Understand your position, Gentleman you are being paid to do a job. There is two hundred and fifty thousand euros ready and waiting as bonus to be transferred into your bank accounts. That should answer all your questions. Just be ready to launch the attack when you are instructed. Are you clear?"

They were clear. Do what you are told. Take the money and shut up or face the consequences. They nodded agreement and returned to their workstations.

Panos returned and sat looking at his screen. He realised that in nineteen days time they were going to take down virtually the entire cyber defences and networks of the UK. The Country would be almost defenceless against Cyber-attack for a few brief minutes. He knew there was no real danger of an actual physical attack and he knew that the systems were robust enough to deal with any real threat to their integrity, but he knew that there had to be a reason for an external power to want to generate so much confusion. He was certain now that Boerescu was not a criminal, but working for some foreign Government.

He felt fear. He had signed up to make some money, not to become a traitor. He had been born in Cyprus, but he had grown up in England. His extended family all lived in England. Brother, cousins, aunts and uncles, all British. He was invested in the Country and he had no wish to betray it. He had become a thief. He had seen the chance of using his skills to dig himself out of the financial mess he had found himself in. Nowhere in his mindset had he envisaged becoming an agent for a foreign power and putting his Country and his family at risk had certainly not been part of the deal.

He looked along the row of desks. His fellow hackers were bending their minds to the task. They saw the bucks. In just over two weeks they would walk away with a nice fat payday. They had no ties to the UK and clearly had no qualms in the matter. He did.

He saw that Boerescu had settled himself in front of a screen. Panos guessed that he was about to communicate with his bosses, a report no doubt of their progress and a reassurance that the UK's computers would be out at the appointed time. Panos logged on and began to type instructions.

He was in charge of the team for a good reason. He was a genius at hacking. On this occasion it required no effort. He had already set up spyware to monitor the rest of the team. It was just his routine. He made sure that they were sticking to the brief and not carrying on any little money spinning projects on the side. It was very well concealed. Even the computer savvy team working for him had not detected the embedded code and they had checked. He had watched them check and he had seen them fail to spot him watching them check. Nothing went on without him seeing and recording.

Boerescu logged on. Panos recorded every key stroke. He captured everything that Boerescu communicated to his masters. He waited until he had finished and left the barn, then he opened the file. It was encrypted. This was a set back and would delay matters, but Panos knew it was a matter of time. He had seen Boerescu check his phone before he logged on. The key he surmised was on that phone.

He checked the network. Boerescu clearly was not too bright when it came to cyber security. He had sent and received encrypted messages, but had logged on the network Panos controlled and had left the bluetooth switched on. The phone had only basic security using the android operating system. Panos was on his mobile in minutes.

The text log confirmed what Panos had already guessed. Boerescu was Romanian. He recognised the language. The language proved, however, to be no barrier. Beyond all sense he had stored, in date order, the encryption keys for his communication with his bosses. With the key and following a quick search of the net, Panos had the required software to crack the messages sent by him.

Panos read. He felt fear and panic rise. As the truth sank in, he knew he could not be a part of this. He had to do something. First he had to stay alive.

Chapter 10

There was chill in the air that night. It was the height of summer but Soo Mi shivered as Oskar shouted at her to hurry up. Perhaps it was the ambient temperature that made her shiver, but the knowledge that Oskar and his two friends were going to spend yet another evening buggering and raping her, that made her tremble. She had learnt the names of her party friends, Kacper and Filip. She followed Oskar down the stairs and out of the block where the female workers were housed.

Outside his car was parked. In the rear sat Filip, while Kacper waited with the rear door open. Soo Mi was ushered onto the back seat. Kacper got in afterwards so she found herself wedged between the pair. Oskar sat in the front and they drove off.

Filip already had his penis out of his trousers and was rubbing himself as she sat. "Suck my cock, slut," he said as he forced her head down. Kacper sat on her other side undid her blouse and pulled her breast from her bra so he could play with her as she fellated his friend.

"She sucks like a fucking Hoover," said Filip.

"Don't hog the slut. Here suck this," he said pulling her head from Filip's penis and down onto his, that he had pulled from his trousers. She spent the journey first sucking one cock and then the other, while her companions swigged vodka.

"We here, now let's get the cunt upstairs so we can have a real party," said Oskar. He had parked outside the block of flats where, on the fourth floor, he lived in a grubby, one bed flat.

Soo Mi followed the three in. She did not bother to put her breasts back into her bra. "Fuck it, if I am to be a whore I might as well act the whore," she thought. It was defiance not exhibitionism. A little bit of rebellion. They were using and abusing her and she could do nothing to prevent it, but she could let everyone see what they were.

Walking down the stairs was a woman and her small daughter aged eight or nine. It was late for such a young child to be up but the women had been visiting her elderly mother who was unwell. She had not planned to be so late, but her mother had taken a turn and it she had to ensure she was safely in bed before leaving. She, seeing the bare breasted whore ascending with the three men, covered her daughter's eyes.

She paused and looked straight into Oskar's eyes. "Filth," she said as she spat into his face. She continued her journey down the stairs passing Soo Mi and her companions. With out a back ward glance. Oskar wiped the spit from his face and headed to the door of his flat.

Inside he gathered up four dirty shot glasses and filled them with vodka. He passed them to Filip and Kacper who downed them. Soo Mi put hers down on the filthy coffee table where some weed, tobacco and cigarette papers were already present. Kacper leaned forward and began to roll a splif. He took a deep draught and passed it on to Oskar. Soo Mi declined the marijuana and stood in the middle of the room.

"Strip, strip," they chanted.

Soo Mi did as she was told. She wiggled her hips and slid her skirt to the floor. The turning touched her toes so they could view the curvature of her small rounded bottom. One button at a time she undid her blouse. Oskar had put some music on but she ignored the beat that was far too fast for her purposes.

She turned her back as she undid her bra. She slid the straps from her shoulders. She turned, hand cupping her bra over her breasts. She removed her hands and the bra cups clung to her erect nipples. Slowly she gyrated from side to side and her bra slid from her nipples and fell to the floor. Her breast exposed again captivated the three drunken men. Oskar and Filip had their penis out of their trousers and were masturbating slowly as they watched her dance topless.

She turned her back on the three again and keeping her legs straight, slowly pulled her panties down. The men took deep breaths in unison as first her anus then her virgina was presented as she pulled the thin material down. She stayed legs together as she took them to the ground. Then she stepped from her knickers and touching he toes spread her legs apart. The tension mounted as she wiggled from side to side her labia open and inviting.

She turned and bowed. There was applause. It was as if she had performed willingly. As if these three men had somehow been transported to a strip club and they were paying for a lap dance. Somehow they had in their minds forgotten that they were forcing this woman to have sex and raping her. Soo Mi they knew had no choice. The threat of sending her back to North Korea and the loss of her pay-packet to the State would certainly seal her's if not her family's fate.

"Let's make it special," she said.

"How," they asked.

"Air tight," she whooped. "Air tight," she began the chant.

"Air tight," they joined in.

She encouraged them further. "All together, who wants my cunt, who wants my arse and who wants to fuck my mouth? Fill all my holes and make me," she paused and then shouted, "air tight."

They were drunk, they were all naked and they followed her into the bedroom chanting. She picked up the bag she had with her as she went into the room. "Lights out," she giggled, turning the living room light off as she entered the pitch black bedroom. "Fuck my holes in the dark,"

Kacper was the first to stagger drunkenly into the pitch black room. "Air tight," he chanted. The chant stopped followed by a groan. Oskar entered and then Filip. The chants of "air tight," were replaced by screaming. Soo Mi turned the light on.

"Die you fuckers," she screamed as she slashed with the hand held sickle that she had been given to cut away excessive vegetation in the fields. It was razor sharp and ideal for slicing flesh.

She had hacked in the darkness, feeling the warm blood spurt from the three drunk, unsuspecting scumbags. Filip had half his face missing and was a mass of hanging meat; it was as it should have been. Soo Mi finished the job by hacking across his throat, almost completely severing his head from his body. He pitched forward and died with no further fuss.

She had completely sliced Kacper's belly open and she laughed as he stood there trying to hold his guts in that were tumbling like a long chain of sausages through his fingers. "For fucks sake, I told you to die," she said as she cut his head off with a massive swing of the sickle.

She turned and stood silently watching the whimpering Oskar. "Looks like your raping days are over for good, you piece of shit," she said. He stood uncomprehending looking at the ground. There, at his feet were his testicles and his penis, which she had neatly cut from him. The blood spurted from the gaping wound that remained beneath his belly.

"What part of die, don't you get?" she asked as she finished the job by decapitating him.

She stood, dripping in blood from head to toe, looking at the three mutilated corpses scattered around her. She felt pleased with her handy work. All that gruelling training in the Special Forces camp in North Korea had not been wasted after all. She wiped the blood from her watch face so she could make out the time. "Fuck I'm late." She stepped over the bodies and made her way to the bathroom.

The water was cold but served its purpose and within minutes she had removed nearly all the blood from her body. She dried herself quickly but not thoroughly, that made it difficult to pull the clothes on over her damp body. Finally she was ready to go.

She dashed down the stairs from the flat and ran to the corner of the main road. She saw the Mercedes waiting with its engine running. She ran to the car, opened the front door and got in.

"Where the fuck, have you been?"

"I had a bit of tidying up to do, sorry."

"I'll have to drive faster than I wanted. I didn't want to risk drawing attention to us."

"I've already said I am sorry. Where am I going?"

He handed her an airline ticket, a new passport and a hotel voucher. "You are now a Chinese Tourist. Stay at the hotel and wait for instructions."

Chapter 11

"So, what did the Triad supremo in London want?" asked Harriet. She, Madeleine and Tim were in the one of the conference rooms in Thames House at MI5's headquarters in London.

"You seem to have a fondness for Zhen Zhou, despite the fact he is a scumbag of the first order," said Madeleine.

"It's a long story, but he sort of saved my life. To be fair he is a nasty piece of work from a police point of view, on the other hand, he has his uses from the Secret Service point of view. As I say, he sort of helped me to continue breathing," replied Harriet.

"Anyway, putting aside great scumbags we have come to know and Love. Zhen Zhou was just acting as a go between and providing the location for contact with Henry Young," said Tim.

"Wow, what dragged him into the open? As head of Chinese spying in the UK, he usually keeps his head well below the parapet" said Harriet.

"It's that time of year apparently, a bit like wasps emerging from the woodwork. It gets a bit warmer and they come out to feed," said Madeleine.

Harriet and Tim both looked at her. "What, too poetic?" she said,

"Just a bit random, perhaps?" said Tim.

"So what did our wasp want?" said Harriet.

"He wants us to stop Kim Jong-un blowing up a South Korean

battleship with an Inter-Continental Ballistic Missile," said Madeleine.

Harriet looked puzzled and for once was lost for words. She pondered the sentence for a while. "I know I am smart, but I am not sure that this had a great deal to do with me? Unless you guys have forgotten I am head of cyber security here. Just to clarify that, it sort of means I deal with that computer stuff, like the internet. The last time I looked, rocket science was not on the job description."

"It sort of is now," said Madeleine.

"I know that North Korea just launched an ICBM and it went about five hundred miles and fell in the sea, but that's all I know about it," said Harriet.

"About all we knew as well before we met with Young. Now I have had a briefing put together." Tim handed a few sheets of papers to his companions. "Have a quick read of these." There was a few moments silence as they studied.

"It is just the basics, but it is enough to get the drift. We all know that North Korea has successfully tested a number of nuclear devices. The US have been applying sanctions on them for yonks, trying to get them to pack in their nuclear programme. The sanctions have had little effect for two reasons. The leader, Kim Jong-un is a tyrant and even if the entire population starves, it would have no effect on policy. Secondly, China supports and maintains him in power. They have carried on with their bomb making despite all international pressure."

Tim continued. "The launching of the ICBM that, as you say, only went five hundred miles has certainly upped the anti. The five hundred miles is misleading in that the trajectory was very acute. If North Korea had launched it on a shallower trajectory, you can see from the briefing, it looks like it would have reached US territory, perhaps Hawaii or even Alaska."

"Yes, I get that and the US are putting on a show of strength by sending a shit load of American ships to perform joint manoeuvres with the South Koreans just off the coast, to remind Kim Jong-un what he is up against," said Harriet.

"In order to have a truly effective nuclear ICBM you need two things. A nuclear warhead you can stick on the top and a guidance system that gets the payload to the effective target," said Tim.

"Reading this, North Korea's threat is less than credible though. They are nowhere near making a warhead small enough to sit on their rocket. The intelligence in the briefing says they do not have the technological capability to miniaturise to the extent required to make it viable. At this moment they would need a much bigger rocket than they currently have to get a nuke off the ground."

"It is the same problem the Russians have. They have been unable to match the US in miniaturising their nuclear warheads so they have had to build missiles that are far larger than the American equivalent," said Madeleine.

"So, all good," said Harriet. "Rocket too small or bomb too big, either way the end of the World is on hold for a bit longer."

"Sort of, but I did say there were two bits to have a credible weapon. The second is the ability to get it to go where you want it to. That, I'm afraid, is why Henry has made contact through the back door," said Tim.

"How do you guide a missile?" said Harriet.

"Well loads of way, gyros, lasers all play their part, but as you can see, common or garden sat nav is a viable alternative."

"Surely that is too risky, take out the satellites and your missiles don't know where they are?" said Harriet.

"True, so the US use lots of high tech methods like contour maps, but North Korea is not up to the alternatives technologically.

According to Young, at our meeting, they are going for a sat nav approach," said Madeleine.

"There are three possible navigation satellite alternatives. The Global Position System is the best, with the most satellites, then you have the Russian and the Chinese versions. GLONASS is the Russian equivalent and with fewer satellites is less accurate. The Chinese BeiDou system, with two clusters of satellites, is even more limited in its coverage," said Tim.

"So the North Koreans are looking for a cheap and simple way to get their ICBM to their target and their plan is to stick a sat nav in them? It can't be that simple," said Harriet

"Of course it isn't. They can jam the signals and deny access. During the Iraq war, the US blocked access to the opposition forces. It is important to distinguish between the US civil GPS system and the military equivalent. You wouldn't get far with an ICBM and Google maps route finder. To fire a rocket to the edge of space and bring it down on the right spot is a bit trickier apparently."

"So the North Koreans don't have the means, unless the Russians or Chinese give them access to their military satellite navigational systems. Don't tell me, Young says they are, surely not?" said Harriet.

"No, that was the point of him making contact. Oddly enough, even the Chinese are not that keen on North Korea starting World War Three on the whim of Kim Jong-Un so they, along with the Russians, have blocked any access."

"So problem solved, no cheap and easy guidance systems for unpredictable, megalomaniac, despot."

"Except Young has intelligence assets inside North Korea. Something neither we, nor the US has and they have uncovered something. That is the worrying bit. The UK, as part of systems integration with the US, has full access to their military GPS systems. It is a necessity, part of the overall command and control structure that stops us blowing each other up when we are operating in the same sphere of combat. The integration has continued to increase year on year. There were too many so called "friendly fire" incidents to do otherwise. The US was actually better at killing British troops in Iraq than the enemy."

"What did Young tell you over lunch?"

"That someone is working with the North Koreans, for a fat pay cheque, to link them into the US GPS system as a sub system of the UK Command and Control Structure," said Madeleine.

"Piggy back them in, with the UK acting as piggy," said Harriet.

"Exactly, we have a traitor," said Tim.

"It can't be done. We or GCHQ would detect it and block it," said Harriet

"Are you sure?" said Tim.

Chapter 12

The time was approaching, his time, the time for the World to know his power and intelligence. He would let them all know of his crimes. He would defy them. He would taunt them. He would out think them. They would all soon know how clever he was. The police, he knew, was no match for him. They did not have his brains. He would send them like some pack of hounds following a false trail and missing their fox.

He had planned his route carefully. He had the tools and the know how to track every camera and automatic number plate recognition system. He would be invisible on his travels. But he, to be twice sure, realised there was always the chance of being picked up on a cruising police car or a manned roadside speed trap. He had to factor that probability into his plan. He had.

The killer pulled into the industrial estate. It was early Friday evening. He was driving his Ford Focus. He had been careful to avoid any CCTV in his drive from work. He unlocked the door to the work shop and passed the bench where he had used his victims, mutilated and murdered them. He made his way to the loading bay where the Ford Transit was parked. It was a tight squeeze past the chest freezer, where their bodies were stored and the van.

The white Ford Transit was no longer white. It was red. The killer was proud of the paint job. Not perfect but adequate. Up close the brush strokes were visible.. Finding the right print had been difficult. The colour match was not perfect, but there was little he could do to improve it. He had finally acquired, bit by bit, sufficient water based paint to cover the white van and turn it red. The riskiest part of his plan was the weather.

The adhesion of the paint to the factory finish was not good. He feared rain. He had checked the weather reports and planned his route accordingly. It was summer, the forecast was a heat wave for the next two days and no rain. He did not like it, but he had no control.

He opened the carrier bag he had with him and removed the set of number plates. They had turned out to be the most difficult part of his plan. There was a time you could go anywhere in England and just get a set made up. The law had changed making the car thief's life harder. You now had to prove ownership of the vehicle, producing ID and the registration documents. A check of the Vehicle Identification Number, the VIN, would soon reveal if the number plate did not match the vehicle and the paper work.

The killer had the skill and the tools and soon located what he needed on the Dark Web. Sign makers that would make a set of plates, no questions asked, at a price of course. The dark web was a name given to an area of internet that was used by criminals and other clandestine users. The killer was well versed in the dark web and had already The Onion Router he required installed on his system. TOR is a modified version of the Firefox browser. It does not allow some of the plug-ins available, but it lets the user browse with a level of privacy not available in the normal version. The "Onion" vegetation reference highlights the layers of protection embedded to try and ensure anonymity for the user. The killer knew that whilst TOR did offer some level of protection from prying eyes, it was not enough to be completely hidden from view. To further cover his tracks he used a Virtual Private Network. A VPN uses publicly available wires, usually the internet, to connect to a private network. This could be a company's internal network. It uses encryption and other security software to keep the user and the data free from prying eyes, such as the Police and Security Forces,

He soon found a garage ready to supply the number plates. It had been easier than he thought. There had been no questions and cash was all that was required. Before handing over the number plates, the seller had been careful to wipe and bleach them to remove any DNA or finger prints.

He attached them on top of the existing plates using sticky pads he had bought at his local supermarket. He now had a red transit van with new number plates. If the plates were run, they would match a red transit sat outside a builder's house in Gravesend in Kent, a man with no criminal record and of no interest to the Police and certainly not on any watch list.

The killer pulled on the sterile full body suit, surgical gloves and foot coverings. The inside of the van had polystyrene laid out to receive the cargo. He opened the freezer and lifted the first of the bags containing the three bodies. It was more awkward than he had imagined. He was becoming aroused as he looked at the body parts of his victims and desperately wanted to masturbate on their remains as the memory of how they died triggered his brain.

He forced himself to resist. He had to fight the urge and the desire to kill that was now raging in him. It was a drug. It was additive, worse than cocaine, worse than heroine, worse than crystal meth. He had started with the death of his Mother, relived the feelings and sexual excitement. Then his first kill, then he refined his method of killing. Then he was hooked and he needed to kill more and more frequently. Now he fought his instinct to grasp his erect penis and relive those beautiful moments as he had his naked and dead victims to use as he desired. Sperm on the bodies with his DNA would make all the effort pointless.

The police would never catch him he was far too smart for them. He was not about to throw it all away for a quick wank. He was too clever for that. He calmed himself and continued to load his cargo of naked women wrapped in plastic into the rear of the van.

Nicholas E Watkins

Everything he did ensured the risk of transfer between him, the van, the work shop and the bodies was minimised. He kept a double barrier between the girls and him and their location. The body suit was removed and left behind as he climbed into the cab. He had several sterile lab suits on the seat. They would be donned as he disposed of the bodies.

He started the engine and drove the van out of the loading area. He then went back and checked and locked the industrial unit. Restarting the engine he drove off. He would avoid CCTV for the first part of his journey. When he was within a mile of the yard of the builder whose registration plates he had cloned, he would not take any precautions with the ANPR cameras. In the cab he had several jerry cans filled with diesel. While he was happy to have the Transit caught on CCTV and lay a false trail back to the innocent owner, he did not want his face caught on the garage CCTV when he would have to stop and buy fuel. The cab also contained food. It was to be a long trip around the Country.

Two days later he was back at the unit minus bodies. He had a good bonfire with plastic sheeting, lab suits, false number plates and every item that had come into contact with the young women. He also burnt the fake driving licence and ids. The pressure jet removed the red paint from the van.

He drove the Transit to the scrap dealers and handed over the keys. He made sure he notified the fact that the vehicle had been scrapped to the Vehicle Licensing Authority. It was a small detail. The van had been registered to a fake ID and address, but it covered the bases and removed the vehicle from the register.

In fifteen days he would have his final kill in the UK and then he would leave these shores forever. He savoured the thought of his next victim and could hardly get to his flat as his sexual arousal possessed him. He had his penis in his hand as he undid the front door and entered. He needed to release his sexual tension. His head was filled with the images of his victim as he masturbated

63

frantically. He wanted more. He wanted the taste of the kill. He wanted their unmoving venerable bodies. Then as the sperm spurted from his member, he had the final image in his head that caused him to come, his next victim.

"I coming for you bitch, I am going to kill you, cut you, fuck you, whore, slut," he mumbled as he climaxed.

Chapter 13

Tim was not impressed at having to sit round a table in Whitehall. In his experience the big meeting, as he liked to think of these occasions, rarely produced anything of substance. Everyone just wanted to ensure that they were on record as having played an active role, hoping to claim credit for a successful outcome and deny responsibility if it became a crock of crap. Today was the Daddy of the all big meetings.

With their advisors sat behind them there were over sixty people in the room. Tim realised that this was to be a serious ear pounding session. At least he was first to speak and would be able to switch off while his three advisors made notes for the next three of four hours. He had brought Madeleine along with Jeremy Hurst, an analyst, who he knew to be perfection at taking notes.

He recognised all those sat round the table apart from the representative civil servants of the various departments. The Home Office, the Foreign Office, GCHQ, MI6 and the Ministry of Defence were all represented. Tim checked that his microphone was switched on by giving it a gentle tap. This attracted the attention of the Foreign Secretary who had attended in person and was chairing the meeting. "Order please gentlemen, let's get started. Mr Burr, over to you," said Terrance Mailer.

Tim cleared his throat and began to speak. "I hope you can all bear with me as the first part of my report is an outline of the current situation as it stands in the People's Democratic Republic of Korea or North Korea, the United States, China and South Korea, which I am sure you will be aware of, but for the sake of the record,

I will reappraise in the light of recent intelligence. The second part will deal with recent events and what MI5 believes to be an important potential rise the in the threat level posed by North Korea and the security and stability of the region."

He paused and began to read into the record, the brief prepared earlier by the section head responsible for the region. "As you are all aware, North Korea has been testing nuclear devices for a number of years and has made significant advances. The fact that they have a nuclear device does not mean they have the ability to deliver it effectively. However, the recent launch of an Intercontinental Ballistic Missile has now raised the threat level significantly and is of grave concern."

"The missile seems to have the capability to reach mainland American. As you can well imagine, this has raised considerable concern. The US considers the main threat in the region to be China and as we all aware they have gradually been building a ring of bases in the Pacific to quarantine the threat. At the present time China is fully aware that the US has a vast array of missiles aimed at it and while it carries on asserting its territorial rights of various islands from Japan to the Philippines, it is measured provocation stopping well short of military confrontation with the US."

Tim paused and took a sip of water from the glass in front of him. "Whilst China is the major supporter of Kim Jong-Un and North Korea and consistently uses its veto in the Security Council of the United Nations to block any escalation in sanctions proposed by the US, it never the less, has no desire to start a war in the region. The danger is self-evident. If North Korea decides to carry out it's oft issued threat to attack the United States, by launching a missile at American soil, then the Chinese rightly fear that this will trigger an all out response in retaliation."

"The fear of the consequences of an ill conceived attack on the US was a moot point until recently, in that even though North Korea now has what a appears to be a missile with the capability to cover the distance to the US territory, it did not have the means to guide it to its target. This issue seems to be in doubt however."

"I have to report that I was informally approached by the Chinese Secret Service that has brought certain worrying information to my personal attention. It would appear that both China and Russia have denied access to their military versions of the American Global Position satellite system. This would deny North Korea the ability to hit a target with any degree of accuracy. They do not have the electronic or engineering capability to manufacture other forms of navigation systems currently employed by the US and the other major players."

"Well, that clearly removes any immediate threat, doesn't it? I mean, if the Russians and the Chinese won't give them accesses to their satellite guidance systems, I am pretty damn sure the Americans won't" Tim was interrupted by General Heathcliff, one of the attendees from the MoD.

"Apparently not," continued Tim. "The basis of the information I received from the Chinese is that they have someone in place, who for a price, will "piggy back" them in on the back of the UK. Being the USA's closest military partner, it is fully integrated into their Command and Control System. In effect the Americans would be unable to tell if it was the UK or North Korea accessing the system."

There was silence in the room as the information was digested. "Taking the floor after me will be the CEO of the National Cyber Security Centre, which as you know are part of GCHQ. They will be outlining proposals to send teams to all the areas of the military and security that have access to the US GPS."

The Foreign Secretary spoke. "In case you are wondering as to the US attitude to the situation, I have attempted to clarify matters. It appears that the US President and the Chinese Premier had a private meeting at the recent G20 conference. The matter was raised by the Chinese, but their response was unclear and still remains so. The Americans and the South Koreans have announced a drill in the East Sea, located between Japan and North Korea. The US is sending the Carl Vinson, an aircraft carrier, the Lake Champlain, a guided missile cruiser and two Destroyers. Seoul is also having THADD anti-missile systems installed on the Korean Peninsula."

Tim continued, "It is essential that we locate and neutralise the leak before the joint US, South Korean exercise starts. My Chinese source emphasised that the North's intention is to target a US Ship and sink it. As I said, NCSC teams are on their way to all your departments as we speak to aid in neutralising the possible leak."

"I have one final matter to report on. We have to consider that the information provided to me by the Chinese may be one big fat red herring. We have reason to believe that an all out Russian cyber attack on all military and intelligence systems may be being planned. We have credible evidence that the recent, so called "ransom attacks", whereby files have been blocked in the NHS, other institutions and businesses and payment demanded, may be a smoke screen for a much bigger operation. We cannot identify with any precision the exact source. We can however say that we believe it is not criminals but State sponsored. Our fear is that whoever is behind it Chinese, Russian or Korean, the information of the mole may be a distraction in order to allow infiltration of the whole of the Command and Control Structure. All I can add is that we are working with GCHQ to try and assess, identify and nullify the threat."

Madeline spoke first as they sat in the rear of the Jaguar that was transporting them the short distance to Thames House. "Do you know what is really going on?"

"Not a clue, but something bad is and it scares the fuck out of me," said Tim.

Nicholas E Watkins

Chapter 14

"It is twelve days until you complete your assignment, then you can collect your money and go home," smiled Andrew Boerescu.

There was relief among the team as they stood in the computer room on a Ranch on the outskirts of Debrechen in Hungary. They had been there in isolation for what seemed forever. It would be good to join the real World again.

"All the networks seemed to have been shut down. We have no connections to the outside," said Chuck in his American drawl.

"That is correct, we are going into lock down mode until attack day. Now I want all your mobile devices. From here on in we are silent. After all this hard work and expense I am not risking messing it up at the last minute."

There were protests and refusals. Boerescu raised his arms to signify silence. "That was not a request it was an order. This gentleman will escort you one at a time to your rooms, where you will hand over all electronic devices."

Four men entered the room. There was silence. The group studied the new arrivals and did not like the look of them. Dressed in dark blue combat fatigues, with black boots they were intimidating. It was self-evident that these men were ex-military and trained. "There is no need for any tension. Please comply and let's get on with the work in hand. These men are here for you protection and to ensure the integrity of the operation," he continued.

69

Panos was the first to be escorted to his room. The newly arrived security guard accompanied him. He handed over his phone and tablet. The guard ushered him back out of his room and Panos watched through the open door as every nook and cranny was searched. Satisfied that there was no further means that contact with outside World could be made, he escorted Panos back to the group.

The process was repeated for Justin, Vince, Lee and Chuck. Each in turn was taken by the guard and their room searched before they re-joined the group. "Please line up gentlemen," Boerescu commanded.

Each in turn was subjected to a pat down search, forced to empty their pockets by the first of two guards. The next guard ran a metal detector over their bodies. The contents of their pockets were returned. They sat waiting. It was clear that their status had gone from employees and gang members to captives.

Chuck had had enough. "I have had enough of this bullshit. I am out of here. Give me my phone and iPad. You can go fuck yourselves." He stood up. Chuck was imposing, standing nearly six feet five inches tall and weighing in at around seventeen stone. He had won a football scholarship in Florida State, but had not been drafted into a professional team. He was imposing and angry.

Two of the guards moved in unison. In a set piece they converged on Chuck. In a series of swift moves Chuck found himself face down with his arm being forced up between his shoulder blades. "Please calm yourself, Mr Blue. We really can't allow you to go anywhere at this stage of the operation, "said Boerescu.

"My name is Chuck Wojcik, you fucking asshole, not Blue."

"Please be calm, this situation will only be for a few days, then you will all be free to go."

Chuck gave up the struggle and the guards helped him to his feet.

He was furious and trembled with rage, but the guards stood un-intimidated ready to deal with the situation. He realised that he was no match for the highly trained men facing him and finally returned to his seat. The rest of the group were now clear that they were prisoners.

The atmosphere was tense and the fear was clear in the demeanour of the hackers. Boerescu smiled in an attempt to lighten the tension. "Please Gentleman there is no need for all this animosity. All we are trying to do is keep it under wraps until the appropriate time. My masters are just trying to protect their sizeable investment."

"Who are these masters? I never signed up for this," said Mr Pink.

"They wish to remain anonymous and you did sign up for this. You were only too happy to take the money. So just get on with what you are being paid to do and stop whingeing. Take the money and shut up. In ten days time you will be rich and you can do whatever the fuck you want."

"And if we don't? Do you intend to shoot us?" asked Panos.

Boerescu pulled his phone from his pocket. He scrolled through and selected a video clip. "Shooting any of you would not be a good idea. We need the Hack to work and we need it to work at the precise time. In my experience dead people make very poor employees." Boerescu smiled, "That was a joke." Clearly the assembled found it less than amusing.

Panos spoke slowly and deliberately. "I hope you understand if I say I do not believe you. Even if we complete the task and launch an all out cyber attack on the UK, I think once we have served our purpose you will have us killed. It is the only logical step. So as Chuck says "fuck you".

"I could just kill you now."

"You could, but your Hack would never take place."

Boerescu faced showed an element of doubt for the first time. "How would you prevent it from the grave?"

"I already have,"

"I don't follow," said Boerescu.

"That's because you are a very stupid man that thinks violence will solve every problem. This one however you cannot be solved that way. I am not stupid and took the precaution of building in certain safeguards into the malware. They are simple things, passwords, the set order in which it is launched and from which work station. Simple things, any one done incorrectly and it goes nowhere. Now, even if you torture me you, could never guarantee the programme would run. I am also intelligent enough to know that even if I gave up the code and sequences you would still kill me. So would hold out for as long as I could, but I am sure you would get it out of me in the end. So I have safe guarded against that eventuality as well "

Boerescu knew that if the Hack was unsuccessful his life was on the line. Fear now was beginning to tell as a small glistening of perspiration formed on his top lip. "What safeguard?"

"I instructed each and every member to do the same. Every sub-routine has the same protocol imbedded. The pass code each member of the team inserted is only known to that individual. I don't know what Mt Pink has done so without him the Hack cannot be launched. We all live and get paid or your masters, as you call them, are up shit creek without a paddle."

Boerescu remained silent for a few moments. "I understand your caution but there was no need. No one is going to be harmed and you will all receive your money."

There was a cautious collective sigh of relief at the pronouncement. Panos spoke again without any conviction, "OK team let's get back to work."

Boerescu was not happy. His plan had been to steal the money destined for the team of Hackers and have his thugs kill the lot of them. He was a gangster after all.

Chapter 15

Harriet was tired as she pulled off the A40 roundabout at Cheltenham, she missed the Travel Lodge and found herself in the retail park. The drive out of London had been horrendous. She had hoped to set out mid-afternoon but had been delayed in Thames House and finally left at four. She had timed her departure to perfection to find herself in the rush hour. She had decided to take the M4 and as she sat crawling slowly West out of London, that the drive to the start of the motorway was going to take her longer than the entire journey to Cheltenham. She was wrong. The journey to Heathrow, where the traffic began to flow again, actually took twice as long as the rest of the journey.

It was late, a lot later than she had expected to be and she was hungry. She had intended to go straight to the hotel but, because of her tiredness, had not only missed it but also missed the fried chicken restaurant located next to it. The Asda store appeared in front of her and she decided to park up. It would do, she decided.

She grabbed a basket and walked in. She spotted the magazines directly in front of her and the sandwiches to her left. She headed to the food first. She had lost her urge for fried chicken and decided on a selection of what were described as low fat sandwiches or the "healthy option", whatever that meant. She was reliably informed that a fruit salad counted as part of her "five a day". Feeling good about her now healthy food selection, she bought crisps, chocolate and a large bottle of cola, none of which apparently counted towards her "five a day", were a "healthy option", but tasted really nice. She paid and added to the Planets demise buy purchasing a carrier bag at the checkout.

She got back to her car and dumped her pile of goodies on the passenger seat. She turned the engine on and the petrol warning light glowed from the dash at her. Her journey to GCHQ the following morning was less than a mile. She knew she had to fill up before her journey back and decided to get it over with. In any event, she would pass the petrol pumps on her return journey to the Travel lodge.

Her room was adequate if not luxurious. She soon managed to make the room go from adequate to messy with crisps, wrappers and spilt cola. Having stuffed herself silly and nullified any of the benefits associated with her choices of healthy eating options, she had a shower and dressed in her pyjamas.

She found her charger, plugged her tablet in, turned it on and sitting at the desk, she began to study the intelligence reports. The Chinese, in the personification of Henry Young, had clearly said that the North Koreans had been denied access to both the Russian and Chinese Military GPS systems and had somehow gotten someone in their pay in the UK with the intention of sneaking them onto the US system disguised as part of the British military.

One thing was immediately apparent. The North Koreans did not have the resources or technology to develop a missile guidance system for themselves. The logical source was the Chinese. "A fuck up," said Harriet out loud, "a Chinese fuck up."

She realised that despite the close relations China and North Korea maintained, it was less than totally transparent. Someone in the Chinese establishment had given them the technology, probably believing that Kim Jong-un was a lot less down the road in the development of a long range missile.

She checked on the response to the launch of the missile and her theory was backed up by the apparent surprising response of the Chinese. It was self-evident that they had not expected the firing of the ICBM either. Harriet saw that the US President and the Chinese leader had a number of meetings at the subsequent G20 conference, where the Countries with the biggest economies got together to discuss the issues of the day.

There was no doubt that the matter of North Korea had been raised and it appeared to have been ignored by the US President. Harriet checked through the CIA briefings and it was apparent that the Presidents attitude and response had been somewhat simplistic. The basic tenants adopted were, "fuck the North Koreans, we'll blow the fuckers to smithereens, fuck the Brits they need to sort it out and get me the Head of the Navy and tell him to send more ships to show these fuckers were mean business."

The President it seems, having given it the matter the level of thought he considered necessary, then resorted to "twitter" to pass his machinations onto the global audience. It was then left with his press secretary to clarify what the President had actually told the US Ambassador to say to the UN in an attempt to get Russia and China to fall in with a resolution to sanction North Korea, and the CIA to deal with the UK Intelligence Services.

It was little wonder, Harriet realised that China had approached the British via a backdoor meeting, between Young and Tim to try and get things moving before something really bad happened. That something bad would be blowing up a US Battleship in the East Sea with a missile, guided in part by the British giving access to North Korea of the US GPS system.

Harriet had meant to go to bed early, but her interest had been stimulated as she considered the possibilities as to who had been turned by the North Koreans. Tomorrow she would be meeting with Kevin and she wanted a definite plan to follow in order to reveal the traitor. She had a list of names. It was a surprisingly short list. There was a much longer list at the beginning with the armed service personnel included, but it had been shortened dramatically when she, along with the National Cyber Security Centre and the

Pentagon, had switched the protocols, without including the military directly in the change. True, there was a longer chain of command as now direct access was on hold for the various services. They would need to ask one of the twenty six people in the loop before they could fire off ordinance. This was no particular drawback as the UK had no immediate plans to start another war. Operating units such as the drones in Syria and Iraq had a temporary command structure that circumnavigated the new protocol and were not inhibited in their effectiveness.

.She looked at the list of twenty nine possible Korean spies. She realised that the list was useless. None of those on the list would have the slightest motive to commit treason. These people where the very people, highly skilled, that were defending the Country on a daily basis against Global threats to the UK's cyber safety.

Harriet then turned her attention to the build-up of hacks on the UK and other major Countries. Tim was of the opinion that these were a red herring to cover the real threat. She knew he had a good nose for these sorts of things and more to the point, a very devious mind. He saw things that other people didn't. It was just the way his mind worked. She decided to run with his viewpoint.

She sat and let Tim's reasoning take the baton. She mumbled out loud. "There is an escalating series of cyber-attacks leading to what and when?" She ran things over and over, blind alley after blind alley. "Where's the logic?" she almost shouted in frustration.

The phone rang. She almost jumped out of her skin. "This is Bernard Waverley".

Chapter 16

Body parts of young women were turning up all over the North of England. The police forces in three countries launched immediate investigations. The fact that the killer had scattered his victims' remains, with no regard for their identities, meant that each force had multiple victims. The perpetrator had made no real attempt to conceal the remains.

Lay-bys, ditches, wheelie bins, field and parks were all giving up their gruesome treasure to walkers, passers-by and children playing. Hardly a day went by, for over a week, before another discovery was made. Fear was growing, fuelled by lurid press speculation. The police were stretched to the limit. Panic was spreading among the populations of the towns and cities.

The coverage, the notoriety and the growing fear was what the killer wanted. As he read the headlines he felt empowered, almost invincible. He was proud. He was confident. He was superior to his victims and the police alike. The profilers, drafted in by the police, also knew this. It did not take them long to put together their theories. They told they police they were looking for a male. They speculated that he would be in his late twenties to early forties. He would be a loner with a possible history of abuse. He would be, that was concerning, highly intelligent.

The forensic reports were coming in. They were bad news for investigators. The victims had been washed in bleach. They had been frozen and stored in plastic sheeting. No trace, no DNA, no accurate time of death, no crime scene. The only information available, based on one body, was that they had been drugged with

GHB, the so called date rape drug. The neck and torso of another suggested strangulation as the cause of death.

An appeal for witnesses was launched in the press and on the television. The police received thousands of phone calls with sightings of suspicious activity. The police had no accurate timeline. They assumed that the body parts had been dumped in the forty eight hours prior to the first discovery. Given that the parts had been spread over an area exceeding two hundred square miles and given the time frame, it was of no surprise that so many calls had been received. Police were sent from forces throughout the Country to boost the investigating team.

The public and the military were drafted in to search the surrounding areas where the killer had dumped the young women. It was a painstaking inch by inch search looking for more body parts and anything that might yield a clue. Eventually, they had all the parts to the victims. The identification had begun. One of the women had been arrested previously and the finger prints identified and the dental records another. One victim was never identified. She, unknown to the police, had immigrated illegally from Brazil. No one reported her missing and she had no medical history. She would remain anonymous for ever.

The analysts plotted the location where discoveries of the body parts were made and calculated how long it would take to drive to each location and dump them. It was not a complete map, but it did achieve two vital things. Firstly, using an average speed calculation, they could determine the time interval between each disposal. Secondly, it gave up waypoints, woods, lay-bys and other areas where missing parts could have been dumped along the killer's route.

Teams were sent out, now with a strategy based on the killer's route, to search for any other body parts. Finally, they located the complete bodies, of three young women, save for a single arm. The three bodies were all brought together in Manchester at the forensic laboratory. It was the closest and the best equipped facility available. The bodies were re-examined in a bid to find a single clue to help in identifying and locating the serial killer. Nothing was forthcoming.

The phone calls from the public appeal were also yielding nothing. Over fifty auxiliary workers were manning the phone lines around the clock. Every lead was followed up, taking up thousands of man hours. Old cases were re-examined. Known offenders were tracked down and interviewed. There was no break through.

Finally the CCTV and the Automatic Number Plate recognition cameras gave the police their first clue. The night before the first body was discovered, a red transit was picked up near three of the locations. The search was on. The van's complete route was tracked from Bristol around the killer's route. It was last picked up at the last drop off point where the killer had left the arms of his victim. The van just then disappeared from the camera network. They had no trace of its movements after that. A nationwide search could not turn up on the movements of the Red Ford Transit. The police could not know that the killer had plotted and avoided every camera as he took the van to the scrap yard, changing its plates and colour.

Phillip Feathering was woken at four thirty in the morning by armed police entering his family home in the Montpelier area of Bristol. They did not stand on niceties. They smashed through the door shouting "armed police," in a bid to disorientate and contain the occupants. His wife and children, a boy of eight and girls of eleven were hysterical. He was dragged from the house into the waiting police van. Forensics seized the van and the house was flooded with investigators that began to search for any link to the victims.

The press had been tipped off as to his immediate arrest. The photo of a dishevelled and disorientated Father appeared on every front page in the Country under the headline banner, 'Serial Killer suspect held'.

The real killer laughed to himself as he read the headlines. He knew for certain now that the police would never catch him. He was far too clever and they, far too stupid. They had fallen for his strategy of cloning a van and leading the trail to the door of an innocent man.

The police knew within twelve hours that the man they had taken into custody could not have committed the crimes. Witnesses put him and his van in Bristol at the precise time the van had been captured on CCTV in the North of England. In fact he, his wife and children had been captured on CCTV late night shopping in their local Tesco supermarket. The police held him anyway for as long as they could to cover their embarrassment and then let him go without the publicity that had heralded his arrest. The damage had been done and the "no smoke without fire" adage clung to him for the rest of his life. His marriage broke down because of the intense scrutiny his family were always under. He eventually drank himself to death, homeless and alone in a squat.

The police had nothing. The killer had them running ragged. He knew now that he was totally in control. He savoured the thought of his next kill as he lay on his bed looking at his bedroom wall, now decorated with press cuttings. He was high on his fame and power. He thought of his Mother, the slut with her painted face and nails. He had shown her. He could hear drunken voice in his head. "I was a model you know, in the eighties. They all wanted me to model their clothes, to wear their jewellery or makeup. I was somebody. I was tops."

She was the tops and in demand at size zero. Heroine sheik, they had called it. But it was hard to stay so thin. One solution was to eat and then make yourself sick. Another was a constant diet of laxatives. The parties and drugs provided the short term solution. She had soon become addicted to heroin and her fame faded as fast as it had come. No one wanted the anorexic junky. She was left with memories, a few trinkets, designer clothes, nail polish, make up, photos, a drug habit she could no longer afford to maintain and a small son.

Chapter 17

The summer rain was falling in buckets, causing the track leading to the farm on the outskirts of Debrechen to turn into a boggy mess. It was seven o'clock in the morning and Boerescu had summoned the group of hackers to a meeting in the computer room. They were in assorted stages of wakefulness. Panos had not slept well and had been up for sometime. Chuck, Vince and Justin had obviously stayed up drinking and Lee, like Panos, seemed fully alert as they took the positions in front of their screens.

They sat in, now, damp clothes from their journey in the rain from their rooms in the house to the office. Boerescu addressed them standing in the doorway with his two security guards either side of him.

"Good morning everyone," he said with a bonhomie that was not reciprocated by those summoned there. They sat and waited for him to continue, having banded together to ensure that they were indispensable, by inserting passwords in the routines they had written, it was clear that there was tension between them and Boerescu.

Having been greeted by a wall of silence, Boerescu chose to continue as though he had failed to notice the suspicion in the attitude of the group of programmers. "You are here this morning as we, that is to say the people who pay your wages and have funded this endeavour, feel that it is not acceptable that any one individual among you is in a position to block or hold the entire enterprise to ransom."

He paused and studied the group. There was no response. Most continued to keep their heads down or focussed on the blank monitors in front of them.

Lee spoke, "You have effectively isolated us. We have no phones, we have no internet connections and we are miles from the City. I suspect that if we have attempted to leave, the two goons that are with you would not hesitate in using whatever force was necessary to prevent it?"

"You are letting you imaginations get the better of you all. It was a simple transaction. You have turned it into a conflict. All we wanted was to make sure that everything was kept under wraps until we were ready to launch the cyber-attack. Now we are in a Mexican standoff. You have the key to the programmes and my masters no longer have the control they have paid for. That cannot be permitted to continue."

Justin spoke, "Well I do not trust you. I want to leave and I have no intention of telling anyone the failsafe I have inserted."

"You cannot leave until the cyber-attack has begun. That will be in three days time. Then you will get your money and you can go."

"Or you will just fucking kill us and save yourself a bundle," said Vince.

"The amount being paid to you is not significant, the stakes are far higher. Nobody is bothered about a few million," said Boerescu.

"Well that is all good then. Let us go and when we are clear with our money, we undertake to email you the codes that will allow you to set in motion the cyber-attack," said Panos to a murmur of support from the rest of his team.

There was moment's silence that seemed to be more like an hour. The distrust and tension was almost a physical presence. Boerescu knew he was being challenged. The men before him were intelligent and knew that their only safe course was to stick to their guns. He knew he had no option. He also realised that a physical threat to their well-being would be counter productive. It would merely confirm to them that they were to be denied payment at the least or be killed at the other end of the spectrum.

"Look, I am trying not to be heavy handed in the matter, but the launch of the hack is crucial and is part of a much bigger operation. You cannot be let go. You need to be here and to deal with any unforeseen issues," Boerescu seemed almost to be pleading with the assembled.

Things had changed for him in the last twenty four hours. True, he had decided that they programmers were dispensable and had planned to steal their share of the money and not pay them, but he had not expected them to pre-empt him by blocking access to the programmes. He had also not expected his masters, the North Korean Government, to see through what he was up to. On reporting back with the problem, they had made it clear that he would not live to spend anything if he did not resolve the matter.

Boerescu's life now depended on getting matters under control. The Koreans, while furious with him, had in any event taken insurance against just the situation he had sparked. He was trying to persuade the programmers rather than resort to threats. He was failing.

"Please gentlemen, all we asking is that we have full control of the programmes for which we have paid. Don't make it difficult for us and yourselves."

"Fuck you," said Chuck.

Boerescu looked resigned. "You really leave me with no alternative. Look at your screens."

The monitor in front of Panos and those in front of the other hackers came to life. Panos was confused at first and then as it sank in he felt his stomach churn in fear. The video showed a clear blue

Mediterranean sky and a small village coming into focus. He recognised it. It was all too familiar. The small group of figures walking through the Cypriot town were engaged in conversation and were clearly unaware that they were being filmed.

He felt his heart leap into his mouth and he began to sweat. Recognition was like a bomb exploding in his mind. "Chryso," he said out loud. He looked around at the others and it was clear that, they too, were as shocked as he.

He watched as his wife walked through the town and made her way to the small shop. The camera lingered on the entrance and waited for her to remerge. The shot was cut. The next image was that of the house where his wife was staying. The message was clear.

Boerescu waited while each and everyone had finished viewing the video clip before them. "Now give me the codes and no more fucking about."

Chapter 18

"You are back sooner than we expected?" Tim was addressing Harriet, while Madeleine was pouring the coffee. It was late morning in Thames House and they were gathered in his office.

"I had a restless night and I just wanted to run my thinking past you both so I got up at five and drove straight back to London."

"Well that is dedication," said Madeleine as she put the cups down on the table. "You can sort your own milk and sugar."

"Weren't you supposed to be meeting the woman from the National Cyber Centre? What's her name? Shirley Worth, that's it," said Tim.

Harriet let out and involuntary shudder as she took a mouthful of Tim's coffee. "What is this?"

"Good isn't it?" joked Tim. "To be honest I found it in my cupboard at home.

Madeleine picked up the packet and examined it. "Best before March two thousand and eight," she read.

"It's fine. It's not even ten years past its sell by date yet. Coffee never goes off, "he said.

"I think you may be wrong about that," said Harriet pushing the cup away from her. Madeleine decided she would not attempt tasting while Tim carried on drinking happily.

"I think you may find it's fine as you just put four sugars in it. Can you taste anything other than the sugar?" said Madeleine.

"It's fine," he repeated." Now what is this all about?"

"I have pondered it come up with the following scenario. Let's start with the cyber-attacks on the UK and Europe. On the face of it they look like a demand for ransom by hackers to unlock files they have corrupted. Only thing is. No one collects the ransom. So we looked deeper and the attacks seem to be coming from Russia, then Ukraine, now it looks like China are at with the latest round of attacks."

"Well it is just the usual group of suspects, nothing surprising in that." said Madeleine.

"I said I was restless and reviewed what we know all of last night. Henry Young, the Chinese attaché, tells Tim that the Koreans are after the US military GPS system to help guide their new missiles. I have checked everything and can't find a link back to North Korea in the recent Cyber disruption. It looks like they are coming from Romania or Hungary."

"So the Chinese are misleading us?" asked Madeleine.

"They could be but why do that? We can't prove it is the North Koreans, but let's assume the Chinese, while supporting Kim Jong-Un, are not keen on starting World War three. Now what they have done is funded a team to attack systems everywhere as a smoke screen."

"I surmised as much and reported this at the meeting with all the various agencies," said Tim." So what's new?"

"Let me go on. I also think we know the when. It has to be when the US fleet is in the firing line in three days. I believe that there will be an all out attack on the UK's entire computer network."

"Can anyone really hack the entire defence structure?" said Madeleine.

"That is not the aim. Yes, everything from the NHS, electricity and gas will all come under assault, but that is the "red herring" Tim spoke of. There will be one serious target." She paused.

Tim smiled, "You are pausing for dramatic effect. Get on with it."

Harriet laughed. "I was. The real target is GCHQ."

"But that has to be the Fort Knox of the Cyber World." Fort Knox is a fortress like structure, where the US traditionally kept some of its gold bullion reserves.

"Not if you have someone on the inside. My reasoning is this. GCHQ is the Governments ears and has the capability to track not only the meta data but every individual communication in the UK and beyond. It would be simplicity itself to track any military communication including links to the military command and control structure. I think, if I had the right clearance, that it would be simplicity itself to let the North Korean missiles onto our common defence targeting systems shared with the USA."

"Basically you are saying there is someone at GCHQ that is being paid by the North Koreans?" said Tim.

"Sorry, I don't know if I am being dim, but why has this mole not done the deed already?" said Madeline.

"You are not being dim. Firstly, it would only be a matter of minutes before the breach was picked up, so they hack has to be when the missile is set for the off, so to speak. Secondly, the only way I think it could be achieved, at all, would be if GCHQ went into lock down mode."

"What does that mean?" said Tim.

"Here is my reading of it. There will be an all out cyber attack on the UK. The mole at GCHQ has given the North Koreans enough information to allow them to penetrate GCHQ's defences. Faced with the prospect of a leak, of possibly all its activities, they will have no choice but to close all external links and test the integrity of the firewall. Simply put, they sever all contact with the World and then test that the link is valid, for example, we here at MI5 are constantly exchanging and searching data with them. If their or our system is hacked and compromised, we both would need to block the interaction until we were both sure we were communicating with each other and not the North Koreans."

"So nothing goes in or out. How does that help the Koreans?"

"I am guessing their man or woman has inserted a bit of code somewhere that is triggered on lock down that gives them all they need to guide their missile to an US aircraft carrier or battleship as GCHQ goes dark.

There was silence while it sunk in. Madeleine was the first to speak. "If I understand it, there is no stopping it. The hack will be launched by the North Koreans that triggers a disruption and reset at GCHQ that triggers the GPS access, they fire their missile and we and the US guide it to the American fleet."

"Pretty much," said Harriet.

"So we know the where, when and the how, now tell us the who?" said Tim.

"I have a list of names. It was quite a long list to start with, but now it is a very short list. The key to this is who has the clearance and the access to pop a bit of coding into the GCHQ defence systems. It could be lots of people and not necessarily at Cheltenham. Whoever it is has to be capable of writing the routine or adapting it and have the clearance to smuggle it onto the system. Not surprisingly that is very restricted. Realistically we are down to three people."

"Who, for fucks sake, you are milking it," said Tim.

"Me, Shirley Worth and" said Harriet.

"And?" said Tim.

Nicholas E Watkins

Chapter 19

There was silence in the room after Harriet left. "Well what are your thoughts," said Tim.

"Kevin Drew," said Madeleine.

Tim looked down at the list of three names Harriet had left, Shirley Worth, Harriet Shaw and Kevin Drew. "They all look equally unlikely. I rule out Harriet. She has demonstrated her total loyalty. She has put herself on the line for me. We cannot think for one second that she would work with the Kim Jung-un and his bunch of henchmen. It makes no sense."

"I understand that but we need to consider the matter. You can't just rule anyone out because you like them. It is pretty obvious that you have a soft spot for her?"

Tim looked awkward. He knew he did really like her and in another time and place he would have tried to turn it into something more. This was not that time or place. "I don't deny that. So you take the lead and make the case against her."

"Let's start at the beginning and see what we really have. A report of a planned cyber-attack on the UK, tip off from the Chinese that the North Koreans are after a guidance system using the British to get it and Harriet's reasoning as to how, who and when."

"Not just her reasoning but good intelligence back up."

"True, but again Harriet coordinated and formulated the said intelligence. Are we one hundred per cent sure she is not creating a smoke screen, to allow her to operate in plain sight."

"So run the scenario past me, how does it play out?" said Tim.

"Well, how about this as the game plan. She is in the pocket of the Koreans. They tell her about their plan to hack the intelligence systems. She uses this to focus the attention of that activity and in the meantime creates suspicion against Worth and Drew. While we are looking the wrong way she slips the code into the system and bingo, the Koreans have the access they want to their guidance system. To support my theory, she is on her way, as we speak, to work alongside Worth and Drew at GCHQ under the guise of identifying which one of them is the mole."

"Bit thin on motive, why would she?"

"Yes, that is a problem, money?" said Madeleine.

"I don't buy it, do you?"

"No, not really, but it was a possibility. OK, let's look at this Shirley Worth."

Tim brought her files up on his screen. "She looks spotless. Twenty years, kids, family and not a blot on her record," said Tim.

"I'll put her under the microscope, round the clock surveillance and turn over every stone," said Madeleine.

"That leaves Kevin Drew. I am not a fan after his personnel attack on me, but I can't really blame him. He is ambitious and thought by backing your predecessor he was on the winning horse. However that doesn't make him a traitor, just an arsehole," said Tim.

"It does show that he is after the main chance. Of the three, my money would be on him. Let's bring his psychological assessment up on screen."

Tim started pressing buttons on the keyboard and poking the screens try to access Drew's records."

"That is painful to watch. You need to have a little patience and stop just pressing and clicking. Shall I do it."

Tim muttered at the screen before giving over access to Madeleine. "It's defective." he said.

"Well one of you is. That's for sure," said Madeleine as Drew's assessment appeared before them.

They looked at the tests carried out by the Psychologist on Kevin Drew as part of the suitability profiling. "There is an area of uncertainty that is concerning. Look, he is described as a 'lack of empathy and traces of borderline personality disorder'," said Madeleine.

"Doesn't sound too bad," said Tim.

"I am guessing you aren't too up on mental disorders?"

"Well borderline sounds like it is not serious"

"I have had a little experience in my former life as a copper and the borderline is a bit misleading. In the US they refer to them as the "rottweilers" of the psychos. In most cases it is not a great deal, a bit of insecurity, mood swings, and reckless behaviour. I am not an expert, but in the Police you do come cross the more violent type of behaviour."

"There is no mention of that in this report and to be fair, the cases the Police get to deal with are by definition the extreme end. You don't call the coppers when your husband is a bit down, but you do when he shoots you."

"You are right, if you are a bit depressed you don't decide to go and support a lunatic dictator somewhere in the World either," said Madeleine.

"Well that went well. We have three candidates for mole of the month and we have ruled them all out," said Tim.

"As it stands we have Shirley Worth under strict surveillance and Harriet watching every move Drew makes"

"Do you know, I am not convinced? We are missing something. It plays too easily." Tim of course was right.

Chapter 20

"I am going to leave you in charge. Sort the various parts and put them together." The chief pathologist said as he left the mortuary.

Karen Bliss had worked in the autopsy laboratory for two years now. It was busy in Manchester, but she had never encountered anything like this before. The killer's victim's body parts had all been sent to the one location from the various mortuaries around the North of England. Her task was to ensure that the victim's individual bits were reunited. The bodies would then be released to the relatives for burial. The situation was tragic enough without her needing to make an error. She was going to be meticulous and ensure that all the parts of the same body were reunited.

Each part, a limb, a torso or a head had been DNA tested and labelled. She began opening the draws to the chillier and removing each part one at a time. She had three mortuary tables. Two had a card with the victim's name on it, the third body for the moment had not been identified.

She removed the torso of the first victim, checked the DNA and the name then placed it on the relevant table. She would continue the process until the cadavers were complete or as complete as they could be. There were still several pieces missing.

The work was slow, but she knew how important the task was. She knew how dreadful she would feel as a relative of the deceased subsequently discovered that not only had your loved one been, murdered, raped and dissected, but some junior doctor had mixed the body bits from another victim in with your loved one. Karen took her time. Her work would be double checked to minimise the chance of error, but she wanted to get this right for the young women who had died so horribly.

The morning passed and the task was not complete. It was taking a lot longer than she had imagined. Autopsy and test had been carried out by the various examiners, organs had been removed and biopsies taken. All needed to be reunited. She found she had to phone the various pathologists, who had carried out the initial autopsies, to double check the labelling. She concluded that there was some truth in the lack of calligraphy skills among doctors.

Finally it was complete and the victims were as complete as could be attained. Karen sat for a moment looking at the bodies arranged on the three tables. No longer busy with her concentration fully occupied, she, for the first time, could see the full horror of what was before her. The reality of these young women's suffering became a reality. Up to that point she had dissociated herself from the fact that these were human beings. She had been focussed professionally on the matter in hand. Now with the bodies in front her, they became people.

These women had done nothing to deserve this. They were the victims of some psychopath's fantasy. They had been drugged, stripped, murdered, shaved and depleted of body hair and their bodies violated after death. Then there bodies had been butchered and stored in a freezer. Finally, having used them, the killer had dumped them like rubbish around the North of England.

These young women had then been dissected and tested by pathologists before ending up with her as a pile of refrozen parts. They now lay naked, cold and alone on slabs before her. And worse, much worse, was the fact that despite all the forensic testing, not one clue had been found to the identity of the killer. He was out there and she knew he would kill again.

The police had come to a dead end in all their leads. There had checked CCTV, hour on hour of it and found nothing more. They had interviewed witnesses by the hundreds with no result. Every lead had been meticulously followed, but even with the largest team of detectives ever assembled on a murder investigation they were nowhere.

Karen roused herself to start the task of putting the bodies in bags for delivery to the mortuaries local to the relatives. She went to the first slab and began the task. She picked up the leg and carefully began to place it inside the bag, then the next leg and piece by piece, with reverence, she packed the body away.

She moved to the next table and again lifted the leg. She saw the perfect, glossy, deep shade of red of the toe nails as she placed the foot in the bag. She was affected by how meticulously each of the girls had painted their toes nails. They all had chosen red.

Karen scooped the second girl's foot in her hand. She put it down on the table and returned to the first body and opened the bag. She carefully began taking out the body parts until she came to the leg and foot. She looked at the toe nails, the same perfect shade of ultra-high gloss red. She rushed to the third body and examined the foot. It was a match.

There was only one explanation, the killer had painted his victims toenails. She rushed to the phone and put out a call for her boss. While she waited she took a small sample from each of the girls varnished toes. By the time the Chief Pathologist arrived, she had the samples of varnish under the comparison microscopes for him to study.

"You are right, the varnish on each of the victims seems to be a match. I agree, the killer must have applied it. I will add it to the autopsy reports and send it to the investigating team."

"Now we can do more. We should send it for analysis."

"What would that achieve? It is nail varnish. There are millions of bottle sold every day. There is no chance of identifying who bought it or when?"

"This is not every day common or garden nail varnish. Look at it again and look at the toenails, the finish, the gloss, the sparkle. It has to be designer. I think there are diamond chips in it. Some top of the range polishes sell for thousands a bottle and one or two cost in the hundreds of thousands, depending on the designer," said Karen.

"You are kidding me."

"No I am not. You should subscribe to some fashion magazines."

"Send it for testing then."

Chapter 21

Panos looked out of the window as he sat at his terminal. The rain had been continuous for nearly three days. Despite the fact that it was the height of summer in Hungary, it felt like the season had almost passed. Grey skies and rain reflected his mood perfectly.

He had only another three nights of captivity before he received his pay off and he would be free. Once the attack on the UK's cyber systems was underway, there would be no stopping its inevitable progress from computer to computer, Government department to Government department, business to business and home to home. He had to admit that they had done a good job between them. In any other circumstance he would have been proud but not today.

Escape would not be that difficult, but of course it was pointless while their families and loved ones were hostage to threat by Boerescu and his North Korean paymasters. Panos had not set out to betray his Country, he had set out to be a criminal. He had needed the money and his greed had conveniently allowed him to ignore the rest. A hundred thousand pounds as a consultation fee had been OK but not enough. The bonus of a further nine hundred had been enough to allow him to close his eyes and ears to what he was doing.

Now even with a million pounds on the table, he wanted out. In any event, he suspected that Boerescu would try something to swindle them all out of the money. Unlike the rest of them, he was an out and out thug and had no moral compass whatsoever. He would take what he could and would use whatever it took to get it. Panos was under no illusion that not only was his wife, Chryso's, life under threat but so was his.

Boerescu was a creature of habit at least or he had been given a strict routine to follow by the North Koreans. He made a daily phone call. This was the only communication in and out of the compound. The internet was still switched off and their phones were still locked away somewhere.

The team of programmers all sat in an open plan area. Boerescu had an office at one end of the converted barn. It was half panelled glass with a door so he could have a clear view of their activities. He was still blissfully unaware that Panos had hacked his phone using the left on blue tooth connection. It was soon apparent to Panos that Boerescu was not the brightest of individuals. He had set his programme on the computer to download and save any and every thing that was coming in or out on the phone.

Except for one conversation, he had it all. Panos knew that the information was vital to the UK's security service, but he had no way of tipping them off without his wife being killed. He had waited for an opportunity to get out while, somehow, protecting his wife. He realised that time was running out.

Panos was not entirely driven by patriotism in his desire to get the information as to the nature and extent of the North Korean cyber-attack into the UK Government's hands. His motivation was also his own survival. He knew full well that in two days time, once the cyber onslaught was underway, there would be very little incentive for Boerescu to keep them alive or pay them. He knew from the hacking of the emails on Boerescu's phone that the Koreans fully expected to reward the team of hackers he had put together. He suspected that Boerescu would not be able to resist the extra five million and kill them for it.

Time was not on Panos's side. He knew he had to act. He had to warn his wife and get her out of there. If he could get clear he hoped he might be able to do a deal with the British, trading what he knew for sanctuary and safety for him and his wife.

On the dot Boerescu picked up the phone and dialled the number that would connect him to his contact. Panos watched and hoped that he had left the bluetooth on. While he could access the phone at will, he needed to get a message out to his wife without Boerescu seeing it. That was not so simple. He did not want an email notification popping up on the phone and warning him that his phone had been hacked.

It had taken a bit of effort to come up with a routine to block and override the phones settings, but it was not a major challenge for the programmer. In spite of his confidence in the routine he had written, Panos was nervous. He was surprised to notice his hands were trembling as they hovered over the enter button on his keyboard. He hesitated briefly, took a deep breath and pressed it, launching the message that would be sent to his wife from Boerescu's mobile.

He watched Boerescu as he talked on the phone. He saw Panos staring at him and waved. He mouthed, "Did you want to talk to me? I'll only be a minute." He pointed at the phone to signal that he was talking.

Panos shook his head, and mouthed back. "No, it is OK. It can wait."

In contrast to Hungary, Cyprus was hot and the day had only just begun. The island was having a heat wave and temperatures across the Mediterranean as a whole had not been this hot in years. Chryso had trouble sleeping, the night had been far too humid and the night air had been static. There had been no a hint of a breeze. She had woken early and still felt tired as she made her way to the bathroom. The tepid water from the shower washed the sleep from her and she felt more comfortable as she dressed.

She missed Panos and was beginning to worry. It was not that he was working away, that was not unusual. For most of their married life there had been long periods of separation while he worked away on contract. It was the fact that there had been no communication from him. He always phoned or emailed. She had heard nothing since he had left for Budapest.

She was in the town shopping and was surprised and relieved when her phone alerted her to the email from him.

"This is very serious, I am in trouble, but I will be OK. Your life is in danger and you must do as I say. Get yourself to Father and seek his protection. Trust only him and no one else. I shall join you as soon as I can. Leave the house immediately and go straight to him. I repeat stay with him day and night. Love Panos xx."

Chapter 22

Karen Bliss, junior pathologist had been doing a bit of research into nail varnish while she waited on the lab results. She was sat having a coffee break with Noel Manning, the boss of the autopsy lab. "Did you know that some of these designer nail varnishes can cost over a quarter of a million dollars?"

"You are kidding me?" said Noel.

"I am not. I have looked online. It is unbelievable. Look at this one, Azature's Black Diamond Nail Polish, it sells for that. It has over two hundred and fifty carets of black diamonds in it," She passed her tablet over for him to have a look.

He took it and looked, "Unbelievable, look at these as well." She scrolled down the list, Gold Rush Couture Nail Polish by Models Own at one hundred and thirty five, I Do at fifty five thousand with powdered platinum, she read the list.

"Well I know what I want for Christmas," she laughed.

"Have you told your boyfriend yet?" asked Noel.

"I am guessing he wouldn't be my boyfriend for long, if I asked for a bottle of nail polish costing a couple of hundred thousand quid."

"Who buys this stuff anyway?"

"Film stars and people with their cerebral cortex absent," she laughed.

As she went to take a sip of coffee her tablet pinged alerting her to an incoming email. "Speak of the devil. It's the lab report on the toenail polish on the three victims. She was silent as she opened the email and downloaded the findings. Noel watched her face as she concentrated, her brow furrowed as she became absorbed in the findings.

Noel was becoming impatient, "Well?"

"Firstly I was right. Each of the victims nail vanish was identical."

"Totally identical?" he asked.

"In type and composition, but there is a difference in the application. The first victim's nails had a more viscous coating, implying that whilst it was the same formulae, it had thickened more."

"It had sat in the bottle for some time and dried out a bit."

"The other two victims were exactly the same polish but newer."

"So the killer painted his first victim's toe nails and ran out of polish. He then must have bought a new bottle. I don't suppose he used a bottle of your zillion dollar stuff to do it?"

"No, that would have been too easy, but he did use a vintage varnish."

"Could they identify it?"

"It is called Celine."

"What, after the singer?"

"No, some model in the nineteen eighties, before I was born."

"And me," said Noel.

She looked at him sceptically before continuing." They stopped making it in eighty nine, so he must have had that bottle a while, that's for sure."

"Well we can pass it to the police, but there must have been millions of bottles sold, so it won't help much."

Karen was not listening. She was busy googling 'Celine'. "Listen to this. This Celine was a major international model and they brought out clothing and cosmetics. She was the darling of the fashion world, all haute couture stuff." She turned the tablet so Noel could look.

"A red head, I like red heads. She certainly had something."

"Something, she was the top model, number one, a global phenomenon. She was on the cover of every magazine."

"I have never heard of her."

"Seems she fell secularly from grace. Usual story, drugs, drink diva behaviour. Says she died in poverty addicted to heroine," Karen read aloud.

"I remember that. It was the time of size zero models or heroine chique. It was the worst aspect of the fashion trade, anorexic teenagers being paraded on catwalks. It was ridiculous."

"Well it seems that Celine took the heroine chique at face value and ended up addicted to it. She still has fans and a following. There is still a lot of online stuff," said Karen.

"This is interesting, there is a sort of cult following of the cosmetics range named after her. You were wrong about the nail varnish, it was called Celine and was up there with the top stuff we were looking at, see." She passed the tablet to Noel again.

His mouth dropped. "Bugger me, I take it all back, that stuff on the victim's toes cost a fortune. Look at this."

She looked. A vintage bottle of "Celine" nail varnish was being offered for sale on-line at thirty thousand pounds.

"I think we need to get this across to the police immediately. This is the first real lead. They now know that the killer has very expensive tastes in nail varnish, if nothing else," said Noel.

"A bit more than that, we know he ran out after his first victim, so he must have gotten a new bottle from somewhere. How many bottles do you think are bought and sold for that sort of money?"

As it turned out, the police would discover, very few.

Chapter 23

It was only nine thirty in the morning and the heat was already beginning to rise. It would be another blistering day on the Island of Cyprus. The Island, the biggest in the Mediterranean after Crete, was invaded by Turkey in nineteen seventy four and remains divided. Many Greek family homes lay in the North and were seized by the Turks when the invasion took place. Driven from the Island, many of the displaced came and settled in the UK.

Soo Mi sat at the café in the little village of Kakopetria in the Troodos Mountains, southwest of the Capital, Nicosia. The heat in Cyprus and the altitude of the village, the highest in the Solea Valley, made it hard going for her. She was not used to the intense heat after working in Poland.

She had been following Panos's wife Chryso, watching her every move. Her routine was simple, a morning walk to the shops, staying out of the heat in the afternoon and a trip out to a local restaurant in the evening or eating with friends and family at the small cottage where she was now living.

It was tedious for her, but she kept her vigilance. Today Chryso was following her usual routine, going from stall to stall and shop to shop buying food. Soo Mi decided it was unnecessary to follow her every step of the way and made her way to the Taverna where she knew that Chryso would end her expedition by taking a cup of the local Greek coffee. She sat and waited and drank the coffee she had ordered. She had tasted nothing like it in North Korea or in Poland. The coffee was excessively sweet, stewed with the grounds in the bottom of the cup. If you drank it before it had time to settle you ended up with a mouthful of grit. It was served with a small glass of water. She discovered that by tipping a small amount of the water from the glass into the cup, the cold water sinking to the bottom dragged the coffee grounds along and speeded up the sedimentation process. This lessened the risk of getting a mouthful off ground coffee.

So far she had to do very little. Boerescu had made contact and asked her to video Chryso going about her daily routine. She had done so and sent it to him. Apart from that, it was more or less a holiday, far better than working as a slave labourer in Poland while being sexually used by the scumbag of a boss and his mates. She thought back to that night when she had taken her revenge. She had enjoyed it. She had enjoyed the violence and the pain she had inflicted. She realised that she had a streak of sadism in her. She liked hurting people. She put the thought to the back of her mind as she waited for Chryso to appear.

Gathered at the table to her right were the two other women Chryso usually met up with. One appeared to be a hundred years old and the other in her seventies. Soo Mi could not have known that they were Chryso's great aunt and her daughter. Both had lost their men in nineteen seventy four. They had been among groups of men rounded up in the North by the Turks, never to appear again. They had lost their land and their husbands and sons in the invasion.

Chryso was taking longer today and Soo Mi checked her watch. She was not unduly concerned as there had been other times when the shops had been busy and she had taken longer. The waiter approached her and asked if she required anything further, she did not, one cup of Greek coffee she decided was enough for anyone.

Time passed, after a further ten or fifteen minutes, the two women got up and paid. In that instant it dawned on her that Chryso was not about follow her normal routine and appear at the Taverna. She hastily paid the bill and went into the market looking for her quarry. She was unsuccessful.

She made her way back to the small cottage where Chryso was staying. She circled the house using the olive trees as cover. Chryso would usually be on the terrace that was shielded from the midday sun by an awning that protruded from the house. It was a rough affair of metal poles covered with rush matting tied over the top, not pretty but functional. There was a barbecue with a grill, a bottled gas ring and a tap and sink. In the centre of the veranda was a rough wooden table with eight chairs set around it.

Chryso, when it was her turn to host, would usually prep the food outside where it was cooler than the stuffy interior. Soo Mi had worked out that the Cypriote's liked to gather with their families in the evening and eat and drink. Dining was late and usually started at ten or so in the evening. The women would sit around chatting with the kids and the men would separate and drink.

It was clear that Chryso was not entertaining her extended family tonight. In fact, the house looked empty. Soo Mi carefully moved closer to the property. The shutters were closed as was the norm during the heat of the day. The slates allowed air to circulate and the thick stone walls kept it cooler within.

She had to check the situation. She did not want to draw attention to herself. Her instructions had been clear. She was to watch Chryso and keep herself out of the limelight. She had no choice but to get a closer look.

She stepped from the cover of the trees and made her way to the rear of the house. As she approached, she instinctively felt that Chryso was not there. She tried to look through the gaps in the shutters. She then realised that the glass windows were closed. The temperature inside would be uncomfortably warm now. Chryso clearly had no intention of returning anytime soon either.

Soo Mi realised that she had been careless and lazy, sitting drinking coffee while Chryso had left. She felt a small knot in her stomach, it was fear. The great leader, their father of the nation, Kim Jong-un did not tolerate failure. She not only feared for herself but for her family in North Korea. They would not be spared. She had to find Chryso and she had to find her fast.

Chryso was walking, carrying a small bag up a small stony trail further into the mountains. It was hot, but she knew that she needed to get away. The message from Panos had arrived when she had been queuing for vegetables. She had been shocked but reacted immediately. She had taken a taxi back to the house and while it waited she had grabbed some clothing and essentials before getting back in the taxi. She had been driven to the junction of the main road and the track that led into the hills, paid and got out.

The path was steep and the stones painful beneath her feet. She still wore the light sandals she had been shopping in. The hillside was covered with rough brown shrubs and higher up she could see goats grazing, sure footed on the steep slope, far more sure footed than she. She was hot, sweaty and tired by the time the building came into view.

The church had been built in the eleventh century and had stood alone, isolated in the hills, a bastion of the Greek Orthodox Religion. The inside was richly decorated with beautiful murals painted on the walls, gilt highlighted the architecture and the carvings. It was hardly ever visited by tourists because of the difficulty of access. Before her families flight to the UK, Chryso had come here often as a child.

She went past the church to the small, stark, wooden building off to one side, partially obscured from view by the rocks and shrubs surrounding it. She had not been here in years, but it felt familiar.

"Father," she called. "It is I, Chryso."

The door opened and the black robed priest peered from the interior. His beard was even bigger than she had remembered as a child. She remembered this priest so well from her childhood, his rich voice as booming incantations in the small church, the smell of the incense, the vivid icons and imagery of the Services came back in an instant.

He was hesitant at first, and then his memory pulled into focus the past. "Chryso?" he said, "My Chryso?"

"Yes Father, I need your help."

Chapter 24

A small boy sat on the floor in the dirty, squalid flat. The room in semi darkness and empty beer cans and wine bottles littered the floor. The air in the room was stale and fetid, the windows not opened in months, the sink over flowing with filthy dishes turning mouldy. There was no food in the cupboards or the fridge. The flat cold and damp without heating.

The boy looked pleading at his mother, hoping for some kind of affection. She was too self-absorbed and high to care or even notice the anguished face looking at her. Her son was part of her burden another item on the long list of items in a life that had not treated her fairly.

For Celine, it was all about Celine. Was she not the most beautiful, the most glamorous and the most elegant of the super models? How dare they cast her aside? She took another drink from the bottle of methadone, it would steady her until she had her next client, then with money, she would contact her dealer and get her fix. She might get some food to stop the winging brat at her feet looking up at her.

"I am Celine, your mother is famous. Did you know that?"

The small boy knew that, he had heard it a thousand times before.

"I walked the catwalks of Paris, New York and Rome. I was the face of Max Factor, the model of choice for the best fashion designers in the World. They all queued for me, for me, no one else, me, only me. I was number one. I was the best."

The tirade continued as the boy sat, cold and hungry waiting for something, a little affection, a little love or a little tenderness. She ignored his pleading eyes and continued to relive her life, her fame but never her demise.

"They all loved me. I was even in a film. I could have been a film star. We could be living in Hollywood right now."

He sat and waited for her mood to change. The lack of heroine would soon kick in. Then she would become agitated, start scratching and fidgeting. She would become increasingly angry, despondent and desperate.

"They betrayed me. They abandoned me. They sucked me dry. They took what they wanted and then discarded me. The cunts fucked the life from me, paraded me and fucked me some more. I was seventeen when they found me. They used ever part of me then threw me aside like a piece of rubbish. They got what they wanted and fucked me over. Nothing, that's what they left me with, nothing."

He had heard it all so many times before, the bitterness, the resentment against a business that sucked in young women and then cast them aside in favour of the next big thing. It was fashion, it was brutal and it was ruthless. It was big business.

"I had my own range of cosmetics. First they released perfume, 'Celine Morning Mist', then face products. The perfume smelt like camel piss," she laughed, a cackling dry laugh as she recalled smelling the fragrance for the first time bearing her name. "Yes, Celine, camel piss is what it should have been called."

"Then they joined forces with a top fashion magazine, I forget the name and brought out my nail varnish. At the time it was the most expensive that had ever been brought to market. Can you imagine that, your mother having the World's most expensive nail varnish, can you?"

He knew to remain silent. She was rambling, reliving, reminiscing, but he knew she would descend into darkness. He also knew it would not be long before some man arrived, His stomach pulled into a knot of fear as he waited. He could never be sure which man would come. Most of the time they just wanted to have sex with his mother, but there were the other times.

Those times when he had to "be nice to the gentleman," as his mother put it. He hated those words. He hated the feeling of being dirty. He hated the pain, but worse was that he hated his mother. He did not want to hate her and he pretended to himself that he did not. But he knew deep inside he hated her. More than that, he wanted to hurt her. He fantasised about it. It was pushed deep in him, he wanted to hurt her so bad.

He sat half listening to the woman before him as she reran her discontent with the World. He looked at the red toenails on her feet. He looked at the red hair on her head. He looked at the small red dress, low cut with her breasts almost fully exposed, that she wore. His World was red.

"This is the very nail varnish. Can you believe it was the World's dearest? Look at the bottle. Can you see, there, there is my name, Celine."

He looked at the bottle dangled in front of his face. It was red. Her name was written in red, but he could not read. He saw the red of her name. He would eventually see the red of her blood and he would be pleased at its redness. He would want to punish all the women and they would be red, the red of the whore that was his mother and tormentor. For now, the boy stared at the small bottle of red polish held before him.

Now many years later he still held on to the red nail varnish, Celine. His victims needed the red of his mother, that red roused him to the heights of sexual ecstasy as he carefully prepared their bodies. He loved to take their feet in his hands and caress the toes as he applied the varnish.

The varnish ran out after his second victim. He bought another varnish and tested it on his own feet. It would not do, It was all wrong, the colour the smell, the bottle and the label. He knew that it had to be the look and smell of the vanish that he had seen on his mother's feet, sitting on the floor before as she painted her toes.

It cost him over twenty thousand pounds but there was no choice. He knew that he could not have satisfaction or gratification if the details were not just so. He knew that the women had to be just as he saw them in his mind's eye. They were his "red women" and they were there for him to serve penance and satisfy him.

Chapter 25

It was eleven in the morning and the women had gathered for a chat in the Taverna. Today was milder and the hills were covered in a light cloud that diluted the intensity of the Sun's warmth. The two women ordered baklava and a soda. The pastry came rich, sticky and running with nuts and honey. They talked as they ate

Soo Mi watched from inside the bar. She had arrived earlier and ordered the coffee. She had not touched it. It was an acquired taste and she had no intention of acquiring it. She pretended to read the tourist guide as she waited for Chryso's friends to arrive and sit in the café after their daily trip to the market and shops.

She recognised the women from the numerous occasions she had followed Panos's wife previously. She had guessed that they were somehow related and in fact were only part of the wider kin and clan living in and around the area. After the Turkish invasion, many Cypriots had been forced to relocate across the Island, moving in with their extended family until they could reform and rebuild their lives. Some had gone to Greece, the mainland or its islands, others to England.

Soo mi left the money for the coffee on the table and made her way outside. She waited for the pair to have a break in their conversation before advancing to their table. "Excuse me," she said. "I believe you know the wife of an ex-colleague of mine, Chryso Koumi?"

The women, both cousins of Chryso, viewed the small Korean with suspicion. Finally one answered," She is our cousin."

Without waiting to be invited Soo Mi sat at their table. "Please to meet you, my name is Lilly Wong," she lied on both counts.

"How do you know Chryso?"

"I used to work with her husband Panicos Koumi at the bank in England. He was my boss so we met through office functions and the odd meal."

"I see, are you here on holiday?"

"I wish I was, no, I was with Panos a while back. I have been working on a project and hoped to get Panos to lead on it. I finally got all the loose ends tied up and came out to see him. He said he was working away and would be back the day after tomorrow. I have his and his wife's address and was hoping to meet. I have tried calling at their home, but there seems to be no one there?"

Soo Mi realised she was overcoming their initial suspicions. She was glad that they did not ask how she knew where to find them to ask about Chryso but they did not. "She is away for a few days?" said one.

"What a shame," said Soo Mi. "I was hoping to do a few girly things before Panos gets back to sign the paperwork for the project."

"Oh, she has not gone far. She is just visiting our great, or is it our great great uncle, Georgiou?"

"Where is that?" asked Soo Mi conversationally.

The interior of the Church was cool and Chryso sat studying the murals. The interior was dark. Father Georgiou had lit a large candle as a centrepiece that he lit every day. The Orthodox Church broke from the Catholic Church in the eleventh Century. It's spiritual home is Constantinople, modern day Istanbul, there are other centres. About fifty to sixty per cent of the members are Greek or of Greek origin. It resisted the Germans in World War Two, the British in Cyprus after the war and for centuries, opposed the Muslim Turks.

Chryso studied the beautiful paintings in the old church. She was thinking of her husband and the email she had received. She had no idea what the threat to her could be. But here in the interior of this ancient building she felt safe. The Saints looked down on her from the walls and the coloured soft light, filtered by the small but ornate stained glass windows, gave her a sense of calm reassurance.

She was afraid. What had her husband done? She knew he was working on a project and said that it was top secret. That did not explain why she might be in danger. It did not explain why he could not phone her. She had followed his instructions and taken refuge here. The hut where she had spent the night was not comfortable. Father Georgiou kept her awake snoring in the next room. She was sleeping on a camp bed that must have first been used in the dark ages. It was a piece of canvas stretched over a wooden frame. It was army surplus from the War.

She raised herself from where she was sat and made her way to the alcove. There she took a candle, approached the Altar, lit it from the one Father Georgiou had set earlier that day. She knelt. She was not particularly religious, but it seemed right somehow.

It was tranquil and the Church conveyed an air of permanence and sanctuary. There was the sound of a small spring in the distance where the Priest fetched his water. A smell of freshly dug earth, where a grave had been prepared by a local man for a funeral in a few days time. It reminded Chryso that, the last time she had been to Church was for funeral, prior to that it had been her wedding to Panos and then the Christenings of her two children.

She felt a twinge of guilt as she watched her offering of the candle burning in the half light. Father Georgiou was here for her but she had not come to see him since her return from the UK. She had been a small child, fleeing the Turks with her parents when she had last seen her Grandfathers brother. Father Georgiou's church was now in the Turkish controlled part of the Island. He had come here and resurrected this small, medieval building when he was forced to flee the invasion.

This now beautiful building was a partial ruin when he had arrived. The frescos were more or less intact, but the building and windows were in danger of collapse. With hard labour and determination he had raised money, shamed the locals into providing labour and over the last thirty years the Church had regained its glory.

Chryso sat back on the cool wooden benches and felt at home. Perhaps it was maturity or nostalgia. After a life spent in London she felt it was time to return to a less complicated form of living. Prior to the crash she and Panos had planned a large villa and a lavish lifestyle in retirement. That had gone. She had mourned their loss of health. She felt cheated when they forced to live in the tiny house in the hills.

Sitting here in the Church, with the sound of the crickets and the smell of pine, she felt released. Life back in her own land with her family was perhaps what had been lacking in her life. Yes, she decided. She could be happy here.

"Get up," said Soo Mi. "You are coming with me."

Chapter 26

The look of doubt and concern on Tim's face was all too apparent when Madeleine walked into his office in Thames House, Mi5's headquarters in London. "You look worried?"

"What do you make of this?" he handed her an old fashioned buff coloured folder across the desk to her as she pulled up the chair opposite him. He stared out of the window, deep in thought as she read the contents of the file.

Tim had read the file two hours earlier and had spent the intervening time contemplating its contents. In his mind he had run a number of possibilities, but they all came back to the same unpalatable conclusion. It was a conclusion he did not like.

Madeleine, his deputy did not read every page, just enough to get the overall picture. "So to get this straight, you have handed me a defunct file, about a dead defector. I don't get it."

"No, neither did I, but does it peak your interest more if I say that Harriet went to the archive and read the file before coming to see us and putting Kevin Drew and Shirley Worth in the frame as North Korean moles?"

"It is curious but I see no relevance."

"Not on the face of it, but I know Harriet and she does not do curiosity, there is always logic. So I, of course, did some thinking."

"And what was the result of said thinking?"

"I would rather you gave me your thoughts first," said Tim.

"Well, about twelve years ago a bod, code named, Ding Dong, gets across the border from North Korea to the south. To cut a long story short, he wants to trade information for sanctuary in the UK. He ends up knocking on MI5's door and Elaine Wilkins, the previous incumbent of that chair you are sitting in, does the deal."

"Correct, but it goes further," said Tim.

"It transpires he was intended to be a North Korean plant. Their plan was to get him in situ and keep him as a sleeper, one of many as we know. Hopefully, as the years passed, he would become a useful asset to North Korea."

"Elaine saw that he became very useful. She engineered his employment at GCHQ. It was a shame, a fake, he never actually set foot near the place. He was though, for all intents and purposes, working there. He was on the payroll, gained promotions and increased his security clearance. She even faked a marriage and kids. As far as North Korean intelligence was concerned, they had a senior employee at GCHQ in their pocket," said Tim.

"MI5 use him to feed bits of genuine information to the regime in North Korea, just enough to keep confidence and other, not so genuine."

"Exactly, he was the classic double agent. Then the bugger dies, nothing sinister, a heart attack." said Tim.

"Game up," said Madeleine.

"That's what I thought, but I can't be sure."

"He is dead. In my experience, that generally slows down any sort of physical activity," smiled Madeleine.

"You would have thought so wouldn't you? But Ding Dong was never really alive in the first place. True he was a defector sent from

North Korea as an agent, but we at MI5 created a whole career and life for him after that. I am thinking he played absolutely no part after he was recruited. I think Elaine was posing as Ding Dong, sending bogus intelligence to them. So when Ding Dong died it made no difference. She just carried on with the scam, spreading false information, mixed with some genuine verifiable bits and pieces," said Tim.

"But Elaine died?"

"Exactly, she died and no one appears to have known anything about Ding Dong. The conclusion is that he stopped supplying intelligence at that point."

"Did his activities stop at that point?"

"No, that is the problem. They did not,"

"So we can trace who here was keeping him going?" said Madeline.

"That's my problem, I can't."

"And you suspect Harriet Shaw?"

"What conclusions can I draw? I have been going over and over it in my mind. First, she is the one that pushes the theory that the North Koreans are behind the Cyber attacks. Then she leads us to the conclusion that a monster attack is building to coincide with the joint US and Korean exercises in the East Sea."

"We then ruin the party by getting a tip off from the Chinese, via Henry Young, their spy in chief here in the UK, that the North Koreans are intending to hack the US military GPS network, to help get their ICBMs on target."

"So?" said Tim.

"So she throws Shirley Worth and Kevin Drew in the frame to hide her involvement."

"I just don't buy it," said Tim

"Do you have any other ideas or explanations?"

"I know Harriet, She is loyal. I cannot believe that she would work for the North Koreans. It makes no sense," said Tim.

"Well someone is keeping a dead double agent alive and Harriet has enough access to do it. Now she has engineered it so she is at the heart of it all at spy central in Cheltenham. If she is a double, she now has the means at her hands to hack in and set Kim Jong-un's mob up as bone fide UK GPS users."

"I need more," said Tim. He could not in his heart believe that Harriet would betray him.

Chapter 27

The red nail varnish called "Celine" was now the prime focus of the Police investigations. It was a strong lead. In fact it was the only lead. Not only was the brand easily identifiable, it was in short supply after such a length of time. The killer had, potentially, made his first and only mistake.

The fact that the varnish had run out between the first and second victims, the Police were hoping that the killer had been forced to purchase a further quantity. If their serial killer had a stock of the nail polish then they would be no further forward in identifying the suspect.

The task force put its resources into identifying every purchase. The manufacturer was contacted, the internet was scoured and Auction catalogues searched. It was not long before they had a list of purchases of "Celine". Then the hard work began. The identities of the purchasers and their whereabouts needed to be verified. The purchasers were scattered around the Globe. Interpol and several police forces were contacted to establish the identities of the suspects.

One purchase though stood out immediately. A bottle of the varnish had been purchased at a prestigious London based Auction House. The person that acquired it was eventually identified and located in the UK.

The Police began to dig into every detail of the subject's life and history. The break-through was quick. Given the amount of Police resource dedicated to solving the case, this was not a surprise, the result, however, was.

The Police soon learned Celine's tragic history. Her rapid rise to super model in months at the age of seventeen followed by her descent into hell, drug addiction, bankruptcy and an unwanted pregnancy. Not an unfamiliar story, but none the less tragic.

The link was of course that her son had been the buyer of a bottle sold at auction in the time frame under review by the police. A son buying a memento of his deceased Mother was hardly evidence to single him out as the killer. In fact, nostalgia and a desire to have a link to a parent was hardly evidence of criminal intent. On the face of it, it was quite the contrary.

Celine's death was re-examined. She had been found stabbed with her son on the premises. The Child Protection Agency reports pointed towards her son having been the victim of physical and sexual abuse. He had been placed in foster care and disappeared into the system.

The Police passed all they had to the profilers and psychiatrists to appraise and evaluate their potential person of interest. The question they needed an urgent answer to was, could the boy, now a man, develop the traits and motives to become a serial killer.

The answer was positive. Her son could develop in the manner that would fit the profile of their suspect. There was a problem to the theory. The suspect had no previous criminal convictions, held a responsible job and was well respected. In fact the only evidence to the killings was that he had bought a bottle of nail varnish that had been endorsed by his Mother.

The Police wanted to put him under the microscope. In reality all there was, was suspicion and theory. There were no witnesses, no forensic evidence and not even a clear motive to investigate him. They wanted to obtain phone records, bank details and physically search him and his place of residence. The problem was they had nothing to enable them to obtain a warrant. They needed to be careful, misusing their powers or not following procedure could result in evidence becoming in admissible in any subsequent criminal proceedings.

They knew that they were in a race against time. The profilers and past experience told them the killer would strike again. The need to kill would become greater with each murder. The need to kill would become more frequent. With each murder two forces would be at work. The pleasure felt from each kill would be less than the initial high of the first. To regain that first rush the killer would need to kill more. Secondly, the time interval between killings would be decreased as the killer sought satisfaction.

Time was running out and there would soon be another young woman killed, abused, mutilated and abandoned somewhere. The pressure was mounting in the press and in private to track and arrest the perpetrator. The Police had a person of interest. In fact it was their only lead. Their resources were limited and a decision had to be taken. The only option was round the clock surveillance, a wait and see game.

There was no way of predicting when the killer would strike again. The manpower commitment to covert surveillance was huge. For example; to follow a suspect in a car would require at least eight cars, sixteen officers, armed back up on standby and a team of co-ordinators. All possible steps needed to be taken to ensure that the person of interest did not become aware that he was a police target.

The same problems were faced by the police as were faced by MI5 in keeping a suspect under surveillance, while you were devoting resources to watching one, others were going unobserved. You were putting all your eggs in one basket. Get it wrong and the real bad guys would be going about the business of murder with impunity.

The order was given. Round the clock surveillance was commenced. The commitment was made. Based on the purchase of a bottle of nail varnish the Police mounted and committed to an open ended operation in a bid to stop the death of another young woman. If they were wrong, another victim would be killed while they were all looking the wrong way.

Chapter 28

The tension was building in Hungary. The team of hackers were all assembled in the farm sitting at their computer terminals. All the preparation was now complete. All that was left was to launch the all out cyber-attack on the UK. Boerescu sat anxiously waiting by his cell phone for the call from his North Korean masters.

The rhetoric between North Korea and the United States had been escalating over the past few days and weeks. The President was promising "fire and fury" in response to Kim Jong-un's threats who, in turn, was threatening an attack on the American Air Force base in Guam. The big question was if: North Korea could actually land their ICBMs on target. The answer would be yes if Boerescu's hack succeeded and their agent, Ding Dong, could link their missiles to the US military GPS system

Panos knew that once they launched the cyber-attack he and his team of hackers would be of no value to Boerescu. It was self-evident to him that the man was a gangster, pure and simple. He had no ideological motivation, he was driven by money. Panos had no doubt that Boerescu would not think twice about taking the money from the Korean and keeping it rather than pay the team of hackers. The big question was not if he would get paid, but if he would be killed by Boerescu and his thugs as well as not getting paid.

Boerescu switched his phone on. Panos smiled as his computer tethered itself to the cells bluetooth. He pressed the enter key on his terminal and the screen came to life. Within seconds he had what he needed.

They sat waiting for the phone to ring. The team of hackers, having worked and lived together for the past few weeks, had built up a bond. Panos would miss them, Justin with his effeminate tantrums, the tough Ukrainian Vince, the little smartly dressed Chinese Lee and the bouncing over the top American Chuck. He had become used to them and now felt friendship and a bond.

They began as the ring tone interrupted the silence. Boerescu grabbed the phone and pressed answer. He held the phone to his ear and they waited. He put the phone down. "It is a go, launch the hack."

The programmers turned their attentions to the screens in front of them and began tapping at their keyboards. Panos sat back and stared out of the window at the fields surrounding the makeshift computer office. The weather was nice and the sky was a deep shade of blue. Summer had finally arrived. He knew that in moments things would become a little less calm and Boerescu would not be so happy.

Boerescu was looking on anxiously. He glanced at his men who themselves were feeling the anticipation of imminent action. They had their orders. On the signal from Boerescu they were to draw their guns and shoot the team of programmers. They had doubts, but they had been promised their share of the money destined for Panos and his team of hackers.

The work continued as the complex series of malware was locked and loaded, aimed at all the major Government Agencies in the UK. MI6, MI5, GCHQ, NHS, Counter Terrorist Unit and every other major arm of the military had been hacked and prepared to receive the malware. Within hours, systems would be crashing, toppling like dominoes as the viruses spread. During that chaos one tiny piece of software would be launched from GCHQ by the North Korean agent, code named Ding Dong, that would give Kin Jong-un his dream of targeting American soil with nuclear missiles. At that point he knew he would be safe from any intervention in his dictatorial rule.

He had seen the consequences of giving up nuclear weapons and bowing down to Western pressure. He knew as soon as the threat of a nuclear attack was removed, the dictator would be overthrown with the help of the US and its allies. Saddam in Iraq and Gaddafi in Libya had been the latest to be stupid. Kim Jong-un was not about to join them in death. Within the day he would have ICBMs that could reach the US and he was within a few years of having the technology to put a nuclear warhead on them.

"Well?" said Boerescu.

"There is something wrong. It won't launch," said Chuck.

"There is a virus in the system. It has taken over," added Lee.

"For fucks sake, fix it," shouted Boerescu.

"It could take days, weeks to track it down and repair."

"Do it now or you are dead and your families are dead," Boerescu was in a frenzy of anger.

"We can't," said Vince.

Boerescu was now trembling as sweat formed on his brow. His men drew the uzi machine pistols from under their jackets and pointed them at the programmers, but were unsure what to do. He knew that if he failed the North Koreans would hunt him down and kill him. The hack had to go out and it had to go out now.

Panos stood up and looking far calmer than he felt and spoke. "I think you will find that nothing will happen unless I run little routine."

"What the fuck are you talking about?" shouted Boerescu.

Panos was amazed at the calmness he displayed. "I have made sure that I have a little insurance. I may be wrong, but I feel that you are not the most trustworthy of individuals. I suspect that you are also a very greedy type of man. I think that once you have what you want, you will just kill us and pocket the money."

Panos found himself with an uzi pressed against his head and flanked by Boerescu's henchmen. "You will run that programme,"

"I think not. Shooting me will not help, will it? You can't get information from a dead man. You could try torture, but as it is now clear that you would kill me anyway, I should only be making a choice as to how I die. I think you would agree that is not much of an incentive?"

Boerescu was seething with rage. His men looked at him for instructions. He calmed himself and waved his men to back away from Panos. It was hard for him to control his anger. He was basically a glorified thug that had hit the jackpot with the North Koreans and now he saw that he could lose it all. Against his nature his calmed himself. "You are forgetting something Mr Koumi."

"I don't think I have. Here is what you are going to do. First you are going to transfer the money you owe us into my and my colleague's bank accounts. We will then check online that the money is in. Once we have our money, you will give us the keys to the cars and we shall leave. Then I will email you the code to put it all in motion. All you need do is type it in."

A smile spread across Boerescu's face. "I have your wife. She will die if I do not phone in the next hour and halt her assassination."

"I think you should make that call now."

"You don't believe me? Fine I will phone and you can speak to her. Perhaps she can convince you." The other programmers realised that their lives hung in the balance as it dawned on them that Boerescu never had any intention of honouring their deal, but had planned their deaths from the outset.

Boerescu dialled Soo Mi's mobile and waited. He placed it on speaker phone and the ring tone could be heard clearly by all. Eventually the ring stopped and a look of satisfaction crossed his face. "Sorry the caller cannot talk to you call at the moment. Please ...." He switched the phone off confused.

Panos extended his hand. "Please allow me." Unsure Boerescu handed him the phone. "Thank you."

He took the phone and began to key in the number. "You had better not call the police. You and your friends would be long dead before they arrived."

"Not the police," said Panos. He switched the speaker on so all could hear. The cell connected and the ring tone commenced.

"Hello," said a female voice.

"Chryso, are you ok?" said Panos. He need not have asked as he already he knew. He had read her email when his computer connected to Boerescu's phone bluetooth earlier.

"The money and the car keys, please," he said to Boerescu, having finished his call to his wife, Chryso.

Chapter 29

"Have you seen the latest intelligence reports?" asked Madeleine.

"Just glancing through them now," Tim and his deputy were having their daily morning meeting. One topic was on the agenda North Korea.

"It is getting a bit tense over there. The Japanese have linked up with the American fleet in the East China Sea. Their maritime self-defence force has now linked up with the aircraft carrier, USS Carl Vinson and the battle group. They are all heading towards the North Koreans," said Madeleine.

"The military in Seoul say they are going ahead with the joint US exercise called Ulchi-Freedom Guardian. It is due to start on Monday and there are over forty thousand troops and civilian support staff taking part."

"Well, if I were sat in Pyongyang, I would think that there was a war brewing. Wouldn't you?"

"Well the exercises are an annual event," said Tim.

"True, but it is looking like bad timing. The President and Kim Jong-un are going at it hammer and tongs on twitter and in the media."

"The latest report I have here suggests that North Korea is going to fire missiles at Guam. They will use four Hwasong-12 intermediate-range missiles and target the Island with its seven thousand US troops," said Tim.

"Well we know why that is. Don't we? The North Koreans now expect to be able to have their agent, Ding Dong, insert a programme into the control and command structure of the UK allowing them to guide their missiles using US technology to keep them on track. We can assume that they will be launching an all out cyber-attack on the UK by tomorrow via the network at GCHQ," said Madeleine.

"It is easier to hit an Island like Guam than it is to hit a moving target like the USS Carl Vinson," said Tim with a smile.

"I am not sure that is amusing," said Madeline. "At the end of the day we seem to be the department with the mole in it."

"I just do not accept that Harriet would be working for the North Koreans. I know her and I trust her."

"There are no possible alternatives. Look at the evidence. She raised the whole issue initially. She got you believing and got herself in pole position to deal with the Cyber-attack. The matter would normally be in the hands of Shirley Worth at the National Cyber Security Centre, but Harriet pushed her into the frame as a suspect and got her sidelined. Next she pushes Kevin Drew into the spotlight. Now you have sent her to GCHQ where she is in prime position to insert any malware handed to her by the North Koreans."

"There is no motive?" said Tim.

"This is not an Agatha Christi crime thriller. It doesn't have to be proved in court beyond a reasonable doubt. We are in the real World of lies, more lies and half-truths. We are here to counter terrorism. We have to go with the information we have and act to protect the Country."

"It does not feel right and ..."

"And you have history with Harriet, and you cannot see what is in front of your face. You are letting your feelings cloud your judgement," said Madeleine.

"That surely is the point. I am here to exercise judgement. We are in danger of doing the classic of getting a suspect in our sights and ignoring any conflicting evidence."

"Except there is no conflicting evidence, we have nothing. Ms Worth has been microscopically examined. Drew had been trawled over with a comb that is fine enough to remove nits from a school kid's hair. We have no other candidates. Unless you can suggest someone, there are no alternatives."

"I can't."

"Then bring her in and lock her up. If you are right then she will be released and annoyed. If you are wrong then we prevent World War Three."

"A bit dramatic," he said.

"OK, it is an over statement, but do you really want Kim Jong-un getting one over on the US?"

"Of course bloody not, but the CIA should be heading this up and helping."

"There is no arguing that, but the president is not in the mood to be listening to his own security agencies. He sees them as ranged against him. Henry Young wouldn't have approached MI5 if the President was of a mind to listen to anyone. The Chinese have voted with the US on further sanctions against North Korea at the UN. They are signalling to Pyongyang their disquiet. The CIA has its hands tied," Madeline replied.

"I will deal with it," said Tim.

"How?" demanded Madeleine.

Tim looked at her and in a manner that she had not seen before in his usually light hearted and often flippant manner of dealing with things. She suddenly saw that he was capable of a far more steely character than she had first realised. He had made head of MI5, not because he was a nice guy, but in spite of the fact he was. She saw then and there he would always do what was right. He would not do reasonable but what was right. The right however would be his unique right.

He repeated himself, slowly emphasising that the matter was closed. "I said. I would deal with it."

Madeline left Tim's office realising she had a lot to learn at MI5. She now began to wonder if the rumours about her boss's involvement in the deaths of the three Russian oligarchs had substance. She wondered about the sudden departure of the previous incumbent of her role and the suicide of the previous head of MI5. There was a lot more to Anthony Burr than first met the eye.

Chapter 30

Soo Mi had hired a car and followed the directions given to her by Chryso's coffee companions to Father Georgiou's Church. She was careful to conceal the hire car just off the main road in amongst the bushes and olive trees before starting her walk up the track to the Church.

She was not used to the altitude, but she was fit and had no trouble in making her way over the rough stone track. She wanted to survey the scene before confronting her prey. Her orders had been clear, she was to take Panos's wife alive and await further instructions from Boerescu.

As she went higher up the side of the mountain, the trees and flowers that had lined the main road gave way to shrub and ground growing plants. As she looked up and further ahead, she could see the steep rising mountains in the background. The mountain goats could be seen leaping from rock to rock foraging for food. The pickings were meagre, but they were well adapted to eating the scraps of greenery that grew amongst the outcrops of rock.

The Church had been built on a flat, small area, surrounded on three sides by the steep hills. Soo Mi realised that she would be easily spotted as she made her approach. She crouched down behind one of the many boulders that littered the area. At some stage in the past, rock falls must have been common as the wind and rain had eroded the hillside creating the relative flat area where the Church had been built.

She could see the church and the small hut. She could see the graveyard where Father Georgiou was talking to a man. They were stood beside a freshly dug grave. The man was clearly the grave digger and had driven up to the Church on a small four wheeled quad bike. He was sat astride it while talking to the Priest and getting ready to depart.

Soo Mi would wait, concealed, for the opportunity to carry out her instructions. The Greek Orthodox called for a quick interment of the deceased, usually within forty eight hours of death so a funeral was imminent and the Church would be flooded with mourners and grieving relatives probably later that day. She knew she could not wait too long to accomplish her task.

Eventually the grave digger started his quad bike and waving to Father Georgiou drove off. Soo Mi ducked down trying to remain unobserved as he drove within yards of where she was concealed. So far there had been no sign of Chryso. She watched as the Priest returned to the hut and went inside. She speculated that the woman may well be inside the hut, but charging in would hardly be sensible.

Soo Mi decided that her best course of action was to make her way inside the Church and wait and see. Patience and doing nothing was often the best way to make progress. She had no desire to put herself in a position where she would end up having to kill a Priest for no reason. The dark interior of the Church was cool and tranquil and a relief from the dry heat outside. She drank some water from the bottles she carried with her and settled into the shadows to wait.

Her wait was approximately three hours before Chryso entered the Church and lit a candle. She watched as the woman before her took a pew and sat contemplating. She continued to wait to ensure that the priest was not about to follow her in. Satisfied that she was alone with her target, she moved quietly into position.

She drew the small hand gun and moved behind Chryso. She was totally unaware of Soo Mi's presence and was startled when she spoke, "You are coming with me," she said calmly.

Chryso turned to see a Chinese looking woman pointing a gun at her. She was about to cry out and scream, but Soo Mi put her fingers to her lips and cautioned silence. Chryso closed her mouth and stayed still. "Move," Soo Mi ordered and gestured for her to head to the door.

As they stepped into the light, Soo Mi was briefly dazzled after her time in the semi darkness of the Church's interior. The priest seemed to appear from nowhere and stood in front of them. "What are you doing, my child?" His voice was rich and calming and showed no sign of fear, even though he could clearly see the gun in Soo Mi's hand. He stepped between the gun and Chryso blocking Soo Mi's progress.

Father Georgiou was an impressive figure and was wearing his full priest's attire in preparation for a funeral due to start in a few hours time. He was dressed totally in black with his inner cassock covered by the full length outer robes. On his head he wore the kalimavkion, the stove piped hat. He was dressed to conduct a service.

"Move aside old man," said Soo Mi and raised the gun at the priest. She knew she did not want to leave a witness, but she also knew that the mourners were due soon with a dead body. She did not particularly want a priest as a witness. That would not be helpful in her abduction of Chryso.

In that moment of hesitation, Chryso broke free and started to run. Soo Mi was caught off guard and turned to follow. Her instructions had been to take the woman alive to use as a threat to her husband, not to kill her. She turned to give chase. There was the sound of a gunshot.

Surprise then pain spread across Soo Mi's face as she crumpled to the ground. The ancient Lee Enfield rifle which had been concealed in Father Georgiou's robes still smoked. He watched as she died.

"Bless you me child," said the Priest.

Chryso returned to the old man's side. "You killed her,"

"Sometimes God requires the lambs to fight. I fought the Germans when I was just a boy in Crete and I fought the Turks as a man here in Cyprus. Now God called on me protect my family and I had to fight again. I have kept this gun since I was a boy. I hope that I am not called on again to take up arms. I am getting too old for this sort of thing."

"I think we should get a move on, the mourners will be here soon and we don't want more than one dead person for them to deal with at a time. There is a wheel barrow behind the hut. Go and get it would you?"

Father Georgiou searched Soo Mi and found the car keys, her passport and a hotel key card. Later, Chryso would return the car to the airport lot and put the keys in the letter box for out of hour's returns. She would go to Soo Mi's hotel room and remove all her clothes and belongings. They would be burnt along with the passport. There would be no police inquiry as no one would report her missing.

They loaded the body into the wheelbarrow and dumped it into the recently dug grave. Father Georgiou. "I don't want to get dirty so I hope you don't mind covering the body with some earth?" Chryso shovelled enough dirt over Soo Mi to cover the body. Soon a coffin would go in, the grave refilled and Soo Mi would rest for eternity.

Father Georgiou held a small service for Soo Mi before returning to the Church. Chryso emailed Panos that she was safe. The next day Panos called her from Hungary. A few days later he arrived at Larnaca airport a wealthy man, much to Boerescu's annoyance, but who could do little about it having lost his bargaining chip, Chryso. He had not factored in the tenacity of a ninety-odd year old Priest.

Chapter 31

"I don't understand?" said Shirley Worth. "What exactly are we doing?"

Shirley and Tim were in the office of the Administration Director, Michael Esterase, in GCHQ Cheltenham. "I want to monitor everything Mr Drew and Miss Shaw do in the next twenty four hours. I need you, with all you expertise in the National Cyber Unit, to interpret it for me and I need you, Michael, to give me, or at least MI5, permission to, in effect spy on GCHQ."

"It is all a bit odd, you want me to let you spy on Mr Drew, one of our staff. To be honest Tim, I find that a bit off. If you suspect someone you should present your evidence to the people here. We are independent of you after all."

"I am not spying on Kevin Drew."

"You want to watch one of your own?" said Shirley sounding amazed.

"I do," said Tim.

"Surely if you have any doubts regarding Ms Shaw, you should just bring her in?"

"That's just my problem I don't have any doubts, but the evidence contradicts me."

"You must be insane. You are gambling on your feelings?" said

Shirley.

"I suppose I must be if you put it like that," said Tim.

"Well it is your neck so who am I to stop you putting it in the noose. I want it clearly on the record that I acceded to your request, on the clear understanding that it was against my advice and that I accept no responsibility," said Michael Esterase.

"Same goes for me," said Shirley.

"Thanks for the vote of confidence. That makes me feel a whole lot better. Let's get to it, shall we?" said Tim.

Within twenty minutes Tim and Shirley were in front of a series of computer screens tracking all of Kevin and Harriet's activities. "Now we wait. What are you expecting to happen?" asked Shirley

"Exactly nothing," said Tim. "If our intelligence is correct there will be a massive cyber-attack on all and every Government department in the UK. It will have been ultimately launched by North Korea in an attempt to gain access to our military command and control structure."

"And when this attack begins?" said Shirley.

"Someone, somewhere here will give them access to the information, that will allow them to use GPS to aid with the accurate targeting of their ICBMs."

"Well let's hope you're right. I will only know when someone inserts the code into the system, that will be after the event and then it will be too late." She said.

Tim was not altogether sure he was right.

****

"Not a lot seems to be going on," said Kevin.

"It will. Trust me," said Harriet.

"Well I am getting hungry," said Kevin.

Harriet looked at the clock on the wall in the computer room. They had their own little facility set up monitoring all the activity and traffic, waiting for any indication that the attack designed by Panos and his team of hackers was about to begin. It was one thirty and it was as quiet as a mouse.

"Well I am going for a piss," said Kevin.

"Charming," said Harriet as he left the room.

She was alone for the first time that day. She did not hesitate and in the time it took Kevin to relieve himself she had inserted the routine into the shell of the GCHQ system.

"I think you're right. It looks as dead as the dead at a gathering of zombies for a wake here. Let's go out and grab lunch at a local pub or something," she said as Kevin returned.

She had expected some resistance from him at the suggestion of leaving their posts and going off site, but he was really enthusiastic. "Great idea, I'm bored shitless. I know a lovely pub where they do great grub. I'll drive. We won't be more than an hour."

Things could not have gone better. The programme she had installed would only come into play when the defences went up against the attack from the Koreans. It was sleeping and would only awake when a specific event occurred. It would destroy itself and remove all trace it had ever been inserted if the attack failed to materialise.

"Let's go," said Harriet. She would be miles away with a bit of luck when the Koreans got the access they wanted.

******

It was two o'clock when the cyber-attack began. Panos and his team had constructed a series of interlocking malware routines that increased in complexity as more and more computers became infected and put up their defences. Their only purpose was to force systems down. This varied from the usual hack in that there was not to be a ransom to restore the users systems. The only purpose was to cause as many system failures in the Government and defence networks. While Panos and his team were returning to their homes, considerably richer, the UK computers were under siege.

"Fuck," said Shirley. "It has started."

Tim did not understand what was going on, but Shirley's look of panic said it all. "What about Harriet and Kevin?"

"Nothing so far," she replied.

Tim was relived. He knew that in his heart he had feelings for Harriet. He knew there was something there. He had willed that she was not the mole. He had been right.

"We are closing down here."

The computers in every department and arm of Government were protecting themselves. The situation was as if war had commenced and the UK was under threat of a physical, as well as a virtual attack. The whole country was going to the highest level of security alert.

Then silence, nothing, it stopped. "What happened?" said Tim.

Shirley looked at the system puzzled and surprised. "It's gone, just like that, evaporated. It's like nothing happened. As soon as GCHQ went into lock down mode the attack stopped. Not just on GCHQ but across the board. Everything has been restored to normal."

"It failed?"

"It depends what it was designed to do. It failed in breaking down our cyber defences, but it pushed to the brink."

"Well that's that then," he said.

Shirley did not respond as she concentrated on the data being displayed on the screen in front of her. She spoke slowly. "There has been some activity. Normally it would take days or even weeks to check everything but ..."

"But what," said Tim?

"We were watching for it and we scored. I am sorry Tim, Harriet hacked the system and inserted a piece of code just before the attack stopped. You were wrong about her."

Tim was shocked then furious with Harriet and himself. He jumped from his chair and ran from the room. "Security, with me," he shouted as he raced to Kevin and Harriet's location. She was long gone.

Chapter 32

There was not a cloud to be seen in the East China Sea. The American and Japanese war ships were happily going about their manoeuvres. On land, the US and South Koreans were carrying on with their joint exercise: Ulchi-Freedom Guardian. In North Korea a group of very happy artillery officers had just hacked into the American Military Guidance systems and were preparing the launch of their Hwasong-12 missiles.

Then without warning, the whole US fleet was put on alert. Suddenly the exercises took on a more serious tone. The timing of the manoeuvres had been provocative with the rising rhetoric between the US President and Kim Jon-un, but there had been no real expectation of any real conflict. The usual sabre rattling and chest banging was anticipated but nothing else.

Reports started flowing in that a guided missile destroyer, part of the US fleet had been attacked and damaged. There was confusion along the command and control chain. The American war machine began to roll into gear. It looked like the Americans and North Koreans were set to start a war.

Urgent messages were flying between Beijing and Pyongyang and Washington and Beijing. The North Koreans denied any attack on the US warship. The US President was not of a mind to lose face to Kim Jong-un and was ready to launch an attack. China appealed for calm, but moved to a war footing, knowing that every US base in the Pacific and there were a lot of them, was targeting the area. The tension rose and one slip could launch an all-out nuclear war.

Then came clarification, the warship had collided with a container ship. How the Captain of one of the most sophisticated destroyers on the planet had not spotted one of the biggest container vessels on the planet was a mystery but he had not. The enquiry would be a source of embarrassment to the US and run for a very long time. At least World War Three had been adverted, but American pride now had a great big dent in it, as did the destroyer.

The joint exercise carried on with the hope that tension had been reduced. Things seemed to be going on schedule and according to plan. The US was flexing its muscles in the region and sending out a message to Pyongyang.

Then things changed again in the blink of an eye. The United States Strategic Command (USSTRATCOM) is the body that oversees the Defence Department's Global Information Grid, based in Nebraska, it provides support to other combat commands, including the US Fleet in the East Sea. Within seconds of the launch of the Hwasong missiles by the North Koreans, USSTRATCOM was sending out warnings, assessments and coordinating a response.

There was total confusion across all the combat services. No one could assess the threat accurately. Following the first false alarm of the day it was hard to make a call that could set the World back on course for war.

USSTRATCOM tracked the four missiles and waited. The North Koreans were satisfied with the launch and waited for the missiles to renter the atmosphere and with guidance systems, in part kindly supplied by their enemy, the US were confident of gaining recognition on the World's stage as a serious military power. When the ICBMs landed on target they would pose a serious nuclear threat. No longer could they be sidelined and ignored.

The missiles where headed for a spot approximately two hundred miles off the coast of Guam. The Island, a major strategic base for the US, combining air, sea and submarine forces. Kin Jung-un saw it as a major threat. The missiles would let the World know that it was now in reach of North Korea. The United States was about to be challenged.

Chapter 33

"I fucking told you," screamed an enraged Madeleine Wilson down the phone at Tim." What the hell are you going to do now?"

Tim was still in a state of disbelief. Despite the hard evidence that Harriet had hacked the computers at GCHQ and let North Koreans piggy back the UK's defence and attack protocols, he just did not want to believe it of her. "I don't know."

There was no denying the reality. For whatever reason Harriet had resurrected Ding Dong, the North Korean double agent, implicated Kevin Drew and Shirley Worth to the extent that she could legitimately ensconce herself at GCHQ. Now her motivation was clear, to aid the accurate launch of a missile attack on the US in Guam.

Tim now had to face reality. He would have to resign and take responsibility. He determined to do one last thing before he went. He would catch up with Harriet Shaw and bring her to book. "Find her," was his parting comment to Madeleine. He knew that with those few words Harriet had nowhere left to hide. The whole might of the Security Services would now be focussed on tracking and detaining her. She was out in the cold, hunted and alone.

"We have CCTV," said Shirley Worth as she rushed into the room and fired up the screen on the desk in front of Tim.

He watched the cameras at GCHQ track Harriet. Shirley played the footage in fast forward until the cameras picked her up leaving the building. Tim noted the time. It was clear that Harriet had planted the rogue malware in advance of the launch of the cyber-attack on the UK. The camera footage had been spliced together to track her from the office, through the corridors, to the exit and her departure from the car park. GCHQ had then tracked the vehicle on external cameras until it went off into the countryside, where there was less CCTV. They were still trying to locate it by trolling through footage from any and all cameras within a twenty mile radius. It would take time.

"She is with Kevin Drew. They left in his car," said Shirley.

"Have we located them yet?"

"No. Do you think they are in it together?"

Tim was not sure of anything anymore. Could she have been in it with Drew? How long had they worked on it? "I just don't know. What now?"

"We just have to wait until they are located," she said.

They sat in silence. Tim was upset and confused. He now realisedo how much he cared for Harriet. They had been through a lot together. He felt that they had a connection. He had clearly been wrong. Had she just been humouring him so he would not pick up on the signs of her betrayal? Sitting here, bathed in his own thoughts he still could not bring himself to believe in her duplicity. Despite the evidence, he just found it hard to accept. His mood went from anger to sadness and back again on a continuous loop.

He jumped as his mobile phone rang. It was Madeline, "we have a fix on her phone. Shall I send agents to lift her?"

Tim thought for a moment before responding. He knew he had to quench the small element of doubt within him, the part that refused to accept that Harriet, of all people, would betray him. "No. I have to do this myself," he said.

"Don't be stupid. You have fucked this up enough already. Tim for pities sake, step away now before it gets worse. Let me deal with it. Damage limitation, we can still tidy this up."

"Tidy it up?"

"You know full well what I mean. We don't need a trial on this one."

Tim knew full well what his deputy was saying. Send a highly armed terrorist response team in, shoot first and ask questions later. No defence, no witnesses, just an enquiry with evidence presented in camera, concealed on National Security grounds and the press gagged with a "D" notice. Years to wait for the results and public interest moved on by then to something else. Nicely swept under the carpet, his error of judgement forgotten as he quietly resigned and slipped into early retirement on health grounds.

He spoke. "It is not going to happen. Give me the coordinates."

"You are a fucking idiot," came Madeline's response.

"But I am your fucking idiot boss the last time I looked. Give me her position?"

She did. He looked at Shirley Worth who shook her head with an air of resignation as he headed for his car. "I need to do this," he said.

Harriet had just finished her lunch at the 'Kings Arms' pub. She looked at her watch. She knew that by now the North Koreans would be in receipt of her little gift. It was time for her to get to her protectors. Drew was at the bar paying for the drinks and lunch.

"Drink up," said Drew as he returned to their table.

She picked up the water in front of her. "That was not half bad. The food was really good. A bit off the beaten track, however did you come across it?" she asked as she gathered her stuff preparing to leave.

"I just did when I was out and about exploring the countryside."

"You don't strike me as the outdoor type," she said.

"Looks can be deceptive. There is a lot more to me than meets the eye. You should have given me more of a chance when I was at MI5."

"Let's not go there. It is water under the bridge. We both did what we had to do. You supported Denham and I had Tim's back."

"You stitched me up, but I forgive you. As you say it is all in the game. In truth you left me a way out and the job at GCHQ not only suits me better, I am a whole lot better off financially. All in all I am pretty happy at the outcome."

Harriet smiled. "I am glad I wouldn't like there to be a cloud between us."

"Trust me there isn't," he smiled back at her.

Harriet got up from her seat and started to make her way to the door of the pub. She felt a bit woozy and stumbled slightly. Drew took her arm and steadied her. "Are you OK?"

"Yes I am fine, head rush."

"You got up too quickly," said Drew.

Tim was rushing to the pub. They would leave moments before he arrived, but time was running out for Harriet.

Chapter 34

"She is not here. I have checked inside," Tim was frantically calling Madeleine from the car park of the Kings Arms.

"We can't get a fix on her phone. The coverage is very poor and her phone is just not pinging off enough phone masts to get an accurate set of co-ordinates to get a fix on its position. She is in the countryside near you but that's all we can say."

"This is bloody ridiculous, between MI5 and GCHQ we can't track a fucking phone, brilliant, fucking brilliant."

"We are doing our best. You can't do this alone. Let me put out a general alert for Drew's car.?"

Tim considered it. He didn't want the police and every other security agency in the Country involved. He wanted this kept quiet, but his options were fast disappearing. The longer he delayed, the more likely that Harriet would sail off into the sunset with suitcases packed with North Korean money. In his heart he was still not really convinced that she had betrayed her Country. He was not convinced that she could betray him.

"Well?" he could hear the frustration in Madeleine's voice. "Tim can you hear me?"

"Yes, yes I am thinking."

"Tim, listen to me. I can't just let this ride. I can't sit here and do nothing. You know that. I understand your feelings, but it has gone beyond that. We have to stop her."

"I know," he said.

"Well?"

"Put out a general alert, but just report on sightings, location and follow. Do not stop. I repeat that, do not stop and detain her. Just find her. Have you got that?"

Madeleine let out a sigh that was audible over his mobile. "Tim," she began.

"Just do it," he interrupted. "Find her and tell me where she is."

"As you say," came the reply. It was clear from her tone that she was angry and frustrated at his stubbornness.

Tim sat in the car park waiting. Drew's number plate details would now be relayed to all police cars in the area and traffic cameras. The Automatic Number Plate Recognition System would be updated on every static camera roadside as well as every in car camera in every police car countrywide. It was now a waiting game.

If the car was parked off-road it could be hours or even days before the vehicle was located. It needed to pass by a camera or have a police car with ANPR pass it. When Tim had raced from GCHQ in pursuit, he had assumed that Harriet's cell phone position would be easily triangulated. He had not reckoned on the poor coverage which still existed in many rural areas. Her phone was out of range of any of the relay towers.

"We have her," said Madeline as Tim answered his phone.

Tim was amazed at the speed of response, "Text me the current location."

"The car is static, will do."

Tim entered the coordinates into his sat nav and drove from the pub car park. It directed him further into the English countryside. The roads became narrower as he sped along. He found himself in an area surrounded by open fields with crops ready for harvest and the odd herd of cows grazing quietly in the summer sun. There were no buildings to be seen in any direction.

"I am here," said Tim over the phone to Madeleine. "I can't see his car or any buildings."

"I am tracking your phone. You are in the right area, Just look."

Tim got out of the Jaguar and looked around him. Then he saw the car tracks leading off the road. It was a farm track partially obscured by bushes and an overgrown hedgerow. It was hard to spot from the direction he had been travelling, but clearly visible from the opposite side of the road.

"I have a track," he said as he got back in the car and turned back onto the track. He turned his mobile phone off as he drove slowly along. The track was rough and had not been designed for cars, especially low cars with front mounted spoilers. The car bounced and the sump guard hit the rocks and ground as the Jaguar bottomed out. The track was clearly for tractor use as access to the fields beyond.

He guessed that there had been a small holding here with a cottage and a small farm at the turn of the twentieth century, but that the land and buildings had been incorporated into a larger farm with the passage of time as industrialisation had progressed. The track had been built for horse and cart and the taking of livestock to market. His car was making slow progress. Drew, he remembered from the CCTV he had observed at GCHQ, had a Range Rover that would have made easy work of the terrain.

Tim caught a glimpse of a group of farm buildings through the trees and overgrown hedgerow that bounded the track. It seemed that the track would take him away from the area as it veered in the opposite direction. It became clear that he was not looking at an old farm but the outbuildings. He could see that the farm had almost completely collapsed over the last hundred years, but the track still led to the site before turning in a loop to the outbuildings.

His car was now stuck in a rut. After a number of attempts to get it moving, he decided that he was making far too much noise with him revving the engine. He got out of the car and made his way diagonally through the bushes to the group of outbuildings.

He struggled in his regular attire of black slip on shoes and Saville Row tailored suit. He really was not dressed for hiking across untended farmland, but he finally emerged in front of the group of buildings. It was clear that at some stage they had been converted from farm to light industrial use.

He saw Drew's four by four parked off to one side. He was clearly inside. The question was if Harriet was still with him or had she made her escape?

Tim stepped out from the cover of the foliage and started to make his way to the entrance, crossing the roughly gravelled yard. He arrived at the door that was closed. He stood still and listened for a moment. He was unsure what to do next. Up to this point he had only be concerned in locating Harriet and gaining an explanation from her. It had never occurred to him that she could be truly guilty of treason.

Standing by the door on an abandoned isolated farm, Tim now considered the possibility that Harriet may well be guilty. He had no idea what lay on the other side of the door. There could easily be a team sent to get her out of the Country, a group of highly trained agents or mercenaries sent to extract her. He would stand no realistic chance, unarmed as he was, of protecting himself.

Further doubt entered his thinking. Drew could be in on the plot. It would make sense. They could easily be working together. He was now regretting his decision to go after Harriet alone. He hesitated by the door, unsure what to do next.

No, he decided in his mind. He did not believe that Harriet would betray him. There had to be another explanation. He had to trust his gut feeling. He called out, "Harriet?"

Silence was the response. He had made his presence known. There was no going back, who or whatever was on the other side of the door knew he was there now. He called again and was greeted by the same silence. He moved forward and tried the door. It was unlocked and he began to open the door.

Stepping from the bright sunlight into the semi darkened interior of the workshop he could make out very little as he entered. As he acclimatised he saw Harriet in the centre of the area. He started to advance towards her.

Then he sensed movement alongside him. He was taken by surprise. He was not clear exactly what the movement was, but it was fast. Then pain, appalling pain and darkness, Tim slowly sank to his knees, unconscious, bleeding from the blow to his head. "Harriet?" he mumbled as darkness enveloped him completely.

Hack

Chapter 35

The clock was ticking and the missiles were in the air. There was only the big question to be answered now, was it to be fire and fury?

The President of the United States of America had the one big decision to make. Retaliate or hold off? The future of the World now in the hands of the man installed in the nuclear proof bunker with his key advisors, staff and the family, who were also his key advisors. This President was grateful that he had appointed so many family members onto his staff. He could not have known when taking office that he would be the President that might be going down in history as the one to launch the attack that started World War Three. There was, however, a very high likelihood that he might not be recorded in history at all. In all probability there would be no one left to record the events.

Kim Jung-un's missiles were on their way. Their stated target was two hundred miles off the coast of Guam. The planes had been scrambled on the island and the fleet was already in the sea off the Korean Peninsula. All the American bases were on a war footing in the Pacific.

The Chinese were on the highest alert and South Korea and Japan were throwing their hats in the ring. The Russians were ready and waiting and it was not certain who, if anybody, they were going to support. Their President was weighing the odds. The US calculations suggested that he would wait and see if China and the US became embroiled. Depending on who was winning, Russia could seize back former vassal states, like Lithuania and Estonia in the West or seize disputed territory with China in the East. If Russia moved on the West then NATO would become involved, embroiling the whole of Europe.

There were reports that Pakistan was on a war footing, seeing an opportunity to jump in under the radar and reclaim territory from India, Both these powers had nuclear weapons. The next few seconds would decide the fate of the World. It had all come down to a dictator in a tiny backward Country who was determined to cling to power whatever the cost. Kim Jong-un needed the US to be the Imperialist threat to justify his autocratic dominance of North Korea. Now, like the assassination of the Arch Duke Ferdinand by a teenage Serb that started a train of events that led to World War One, another non entity on the World stage was about to trigger a series of events that could the lead the World into Global conflict.

Time was moving. The decision had to be made. For once the President hesitated. He was known to be impulsive, unpredictable and rash in his statements and actions. On this occasion, in this moment, he was the opposite. It is doubtful if any man could ever be prepared to take a decision that might cause the deaths of millions. That was what was called for at this precise moment in time by the leader of the free World.

The Military were divided. Some believed that the North Koreans were further advanced with the miniaturisation of nuclear warheads and that it was only a matter of time before Kim Jong-un had nuclear ICBMs that could target the US. They urged an all-out response on the dictator. They argued that while, in all probability, such an attack would provoke an all-out response from the North and that thousands, if not millions, would be killed, the South Korean threat would be removed with minimum US loss of personnel.

The opposing camp argued that China would take the opportunity to attack the US bases that ringed their country from Guam to the Philippines to Japan. In doing so they would gain dominance in the Pacific and neutralise US influence in the region. The Generals understood that a potential conflict with China would be catastrophic to US interests.

The clock moved another half a minute. The President was the focus of the World's attention. They waited for the order. There was no more to be said. There was no diplomatic option. The US had tried dialogue. The Defence Secretary had been rebuffed at conference only days earlier. Kim Jung-un was not seeing a diplomatic solution. He was out to keep his strangle hold on the people of North Korea and maintain his dynasty. It would not serve him one jot to renounce his nuclear programme. He had seen what had happened to Gadalfi and Saddam Hussein when they had bowed to pressure and stopped their nuclear programmes. He had no intention of being overthrown by the West and executed.

"Well?"

Silence

"Mr President we await your orders/"

It was clear that there was an internal struggle taking place. He was naturally aggressive and gung ho. He was, however, primarily a businessman. Ruthlessness and aggression was a key attribute in that world, but it did not usually involve the potential deaths of hundreds and thousands of people.

The room was silent, waiting, anticipating and fearful. He rose from his seat. There was a look of defiance on his face. He would resort to try. He had promised to make America great again. He would keep that promise. The US of A would not be pushed about by some tin pot dictator in a piss pot Country.

He opened his mouth and took a deep intake of breath. He was aware that this moment would be reported in history and he wanted the words that were to be written, to be the words of a great and powerful man. Not the weary, ramblings of a seventy year old, meekly forced into a corner.

The President was about to give the order to intercept the missiles and attack North Korea. A voice loud and dominant suddenly broke the silence. It was clear and unequivocal and it came from the Director of the CIA. "Do fuck all."

Chapter 36

The dark interior of the industrial unit was filled with light as Kevin turned on the lights. He could now clearly see Tim lying on the floor by the door, blood seeping from the wound to his head, dark and sticky spreading out in an arc around him. He carefully grasped the limp body by the ankles and dragged it away from the door where he had fallen, struck by the hammer wielded by Kevin.

Kevin checked that the door was secure before resuming his task in hand. He went to the bench and picked up the bottle of "Celine" nail polish. He had gone through a great deal of trouble and expense to acquire it. He handled it with a reverence that a priest would reserve for a religious relic, a treasure, an Icon. To him it was all of those things.

It was his connection to Celine, his mother, the super model. He would sit on the floor of the chaotic, dirty flat in which they lived and watch her prepare herself for her visitors. She would talk to him, sometimes slurred from drink and sometimes in an almost hysterical, hyper-active voice driven by crack or crystal-meth. The mantra was always the same. "Your Mother was the Worlds most famous model. I was beautiful, princess and Kings would court me. I walked red carpets. I was the one."

The small boy would sit there listening to the rambling, neglected, hungry and about to be abused. Now a physical wreck, addicted and rejected, his Mother would relive a life that had long since passed. "This is my nail varnish," she would tell him. "My nail varnish made for me and named for me. The rich and famous film stars use this varnish. They all want to be Celine, you see?"

162

He sat still watching as the ritual was played out. First she would remove the remains of the old varnish. Then put cotton wool between her toes to separate them. She would buff and manicure each nail before applying the first coat. It was a ritual. It was the precursor to her selling herself and sometimes him. To her these men were her acolytes, her followers, her worshippers. She was not selling their bodies. She was being revered as Celine, the super model.

The small boy felt fear, bemusement and anticipation. His mother's constant mantra seemed to paint a different World of glamour and beauty. He wanted to believe that vision and not the reality of a broken down, mentally ill, junkie selling herself in a squalid one bed flat. The illusion was soon shattered as the punters arrived. His feelings for his mother became that of hate and that hate grew as the neglect grew. That hate grew so big that it consumed him. It was the hate that caused his hunger and rage. He wanted to kill the red women and then he felt the power within.

He picked up Harriet's foot and gently held it in his hand. He caressed it and bent his mouth to her toes. He kissed them one by one. He ran his tongue over them and between them and gently sucked.

She was on her back strapped to a geological table. She was naked on her back, strapped down, her feet in stirrups her legs spread apart. Kevin had prepared for this for a long time. It was all consuming. He had sourced the old birthing table, the nail varnish, the isolated farm unit, all with one aim, to kill the woman now helpless and at his mercy. Harriet had made him look a fool. She had humiliated him. She had resurrected the demon in him, the demon that needed to be fed. He had contained it. She had released it in that hotel in the Strand. She was the red woman. He had been forced to kill, and then kill again. It sustained the demon, but he knew that Harriet was the only one that could truly satisfy the hunger.

He looked down at her. He looked at her shaved bare body. Her legs were open, ready to receive him. He had shaved her head and all her body hair. She had to be just right. Celine had been a red head. Harriet was the red woman and he needed to complete the tableau.

He crossed the stone floor of the old industrial unit. He then carefully removed all his clothing. He was aroused, the demon forcing him on. He took the wig from the stand. The red hair was the style Celine always sported. He gently put the hair to his face, caressing it lovingly. He then picked up the brush and returned to the naked woman.

She stirred as he lifted her head to put the wig in place. She was struggling to remember what had happened. She had left the Kings Arms. The daylight had been intense as she left the dark interior of the bar, far brighter than it should have been.

In the car park of the pub she had felt strange, slightly light headed and her movements seemed detached as if she was working her body from another place, remotely. She stumbled slightly. Kevin took her arm.

"Are you OK?"

"I am fine," she said.

"Perhaps you had too much to drink?"

She put it down to that briefly and then she remembered that she only had water. It had been bottled water. Water that Kevin had poured into the glass for her at the bar then brought over to her.

Her legs no longer seemed to be her own. She was aware that Kevin was loading her into his off roader. She knew something was wrong as she could no longer control her body. Her mind raced. Was this to do with her hacking into the system in GCHQ and planting the programme for the North Koreans? Has Kevin been watching her? Had she been discovered and was now to be quietly

164

disposed of to avoid embarrassment?

"Where am I?" she said as she struggled to understand her situation. The effects of the date rape drug, rohypnol was beginning to wear off.

Kevin said nothing. She gradually became aware of her situation. She saw her legs hoisted up in the air, spread wide, her labia on display and totally naked. She saw Kevin looking down at her, naked, aroused and wide eyed. He had the appearance of a man in ecstasy. It was though he was in a state of grace, in a place far away and almost religious in his passion.

She started to scream. He punched her in her face. He said nothing. He cared nothing. He enjoyed the blood and the broken flesh. He wanted her to struggle and scream. He would enjoy punishing her, this woman in red, red hair, red toe nails, this Celine.

He was euphoric. He felt the power, the power he never had as a small boy forced to watch his mother in her drunken ramblings, forced to take her abuse and neglect. Now he had the power and it felt right. It transcended all, it was life itself. He was the master.

She lay still. She knew to scream further would only afford the monster more pleasure as he punished her. It would drive his desire higher and harder. She knew this was nothing to do with espionage and the Koreans. She knew she was to die in some unfathomable world of Kevin's psyche. She was the sacrifice in a ritual that had grown in his mind, until now he was totally consumed in the fantasy with no way back to reality for him.

He went to the bench and picked up the long knife, a carving knife that he had sharpened over and over, so now it was as keen as a razor. He had taken such pleasure in its honing, feeling its cool steel blade, shiny and flawless. Soon it would serve. Its blade would drip with blood, red warm, red, red blood.

He stood at the foot of the table, admiring her naked body, his penis waiting to enter her. It was as he had imagined it. It was all coming together in this one moment in time. He let out a howl, a primeval cry that came from deep within him.

"Die you fucking bitch," he raised the knife.

Chapter 37

Tim lay still in the crisp white bed sheets. Save for the constant beep of the monitor there was silence. He was in the Neurosurgery Department of Southmead Hospital in Bristol. They had operated on his brain. He was fortunate to the extent that the expertise had been within air ambulance distance of the industrial estate where Drew had hit him with the metal bar, fracturing his skull. The hospital had over twelve neurological, consultants, leading experts in their field.

They had taken him straight into theatre on his arrival. Part of his skull had been removed to accommodate the swelling and relieve the pressure caused by the force of the blow. They had placed him in an induced coma. Now it was a wait and see game. They would allow him to come round when his condition stabilised. There had been bleeding onto the brain. There was no way of predicting how much damage had been caused, only time would tell.

Madeleine sat on the chair by the side of his bed. She was looking down at Tim's unmoving body, head bandaged, drips, monitors and tubes festooned him as he lay sleeping. She was in a state of emotional turmoil. Was this her fault? Could she, should she have done more?

True, Tim had been insistent on Harriet's innocence, but she knew at the time that it was misplaced loyalty on his part. He should never have gone after Harriet and Drew without backup. She should not have let that happen.

Even at the stage when he was approaching the location where

167

Drew was she could have intervened. She did not. She waited, waited for this to happen. The guilt and remorse flooded her body and tears filled her eyes. Tim looked so venerable, lying in the bed all alone fighting for life.

She had given Tim the location of Drew's vehicle. He had gone to the location alone. He was loyal to his staff, refusing to believe that Harriet would betray her Country, would betray him. He believed in her.

The police had Drew under surveillance day and night. It was after all their only suspect in the recent serial killings. They had traced the purchase of the Celine nail varnish to him. They had discovered the connection to Celine. She was Katherine Drew his mother. They followed him round the clock.

They had no evidence. They could not get a warrant to search his flat or the industrial unit where he killed, dissected his victim's bodies and stored them in the chest freezer before scattering their body parts around the countryside. They had suspicions, but suspicion does not get a conviction. They could only watch and wait for the next killing.

The police had watched as Drew left the gates of GCHQ with Harriet in the passenger seat and travel to the Kings Arms for lunch. The officers had been in the bar. The unmarked car had been in the car park. They followed him and Harriet as he drove from the pub. She had looked unsteady as they left. The officers in the pub reported that she had not been drinking. That was not enough to detain him or raid his premises. An unsteady female leaving a pub with a male was no grounds for a warrant.

The police had been following Drew for days and when he turned out of the Kings Arms, they knew where he was heading. They had followed him to the farm many times before. They knew all about the industrial unit he had rented and they desperately wanted to search it. They had no probable cause to do so. All they could do was watch and wait.

Things changed. Tim put a trace on Drew's four by four when he discovered Harriet had left GCHQ after inserting a hack for the North Korean's into the Military Command and Control network. Tim had been forced to accept that she was a double agent. Even then he had wanted to stand by her and, instead of handing it to the MI5 agents in the field to hunt her down, he had gone after her himself, alone.

When they had lost the track on Harriet's mobile phone, after she left the pub Tim, had requested a bulletin be sent to all services to see if Drew's car had been spotted. Madeline received an immediate response from the Police surveillance team as soon as Drew's registration appeared on the screen in their car. They were parked up, concealed from the road, watching the farm where Drew and Harriet had just entered the industrial unit. She was staggering and being helped inside by him.

The police watched as Tim arrived, abandoned the Jaguar which had become bogged down on the track and ran to the unit. Madeline had lost contact with Tim. His mobile phone had no reception. She had been unsure what to do.

She knew Tim was alone without backup. She had his instructions, he wanted to speak to Harriet, to give her a chance to explain. He could still not believe that she had betrayed him. He needed answers.

So Madeline delayed. Now, as Tim lay in the bed before her, close to death, she regretted that hesitation. A few moments sooner would have changed the outcome. Finally she ordered the police into the building. At last they would get their chance to inspect Drew's premises. MI5 had given them the legitimacy they needed to raid the industrial unit.

The two undercover policemen had raced from the car to the door Tim had entered fifteen minutes earlier. They were prepared, one carried the heavy ram. They did not pause or observe necessities. The door was smashed open in seconds and they forced it open and entered.

Nothing could have prepared them for the scene that confronted them on the other side of the old, creaky, wooded barn door. They were shocked and stopped frozen with horror, their brains struggling to take in the tableau before them. On a chair, legs and body strapped to a medical examination chair, was a beautiful woman with brilliant red hair. Stood above her, a naked man in a full state of arousal, about to penetrate with his penis and with a knife held high, poised to hack her white soft body to pieces.

The moment seemed frozen in time. Drew was struggling to comprehend the interruption. His mind was in a far away place. He was back in that squalid flat with his Mother. He was killing his demons and satisfying his lust. He was feeling powerful beyond life itself. He was in a place of ecstasy and euphoria. He was insane.

As the knife was beginning its downward thrust it stopped. Drew convulsed and fell to the floor. He lay on the ground shaking for a few seconds. Two wires, imbedded in his naked body led back to the taser. The policeman kept pulling the trigger, shocking him as he lay on the floor.

"Fucker," screamed the second of the pair, still holding the battering ram used to open the door and ran towards Drew's fitting body. He raised the ram and was about to bring it down on his head. Only his colleague's screams prevented Drew's murder. He kicked the naked man in the face, the body and the genitals. He was eventually stopped.

When Drew was in handcuffs, they at last had time to survey the sheer grotesque extent of the serial Killer's operation. Then they found Tim dragged into the shadows, head split open, lying in his own blood. The emergency response was quick. Tim was assessed and flown to Bristol and Harriet taken to the local hospital.

Madeline got up from Tim's bedside and made her way from the room. She knew who was to blame for this and, leaving the building, made her way to the Bristol Office of MI5. The Agency now had outposts all around England, Scotland, Wales and Northern Ireland. The terrorist bombing in London in July two thousand and five had changed how MI5 operated and the Agency had expanded its operations and offices thought the regions and increased its staff from around two to three thousand. This would be Madeline's first visit to the Bristol office.

Chapter 38

Harriet sat in the interrogation room. She had been collected from the hospital and delivered to the Bristol office of MI5. Madeline entered, a look of utter disdain on her face. "How is Tim?" she asked.

"What do you care?"

"I do care, I really care," she said with tears in her eyes.

"I can see that. Perhaps you should have cared a little more before you sold out to Kim Jung-un and his bunch of psychos."

"I did not sell out?"

"Don't give me that shit. You uploaded a programme to allow them to get their fucking missiles flying to Guam. You used an old asset, a double agent we called Ding Dong to cover you tracks. Just don't bother with the lies. I am only here to ask you one question. We know you are guilty but why?"

Harriet started to speak. "It goes back four days when I was in Cheltenham at the hotel near GCHQ. The next day I was to meet with Drew and Shirley Worth."

******

Her mobile phone rang. She recognised the number.

"I am in bed," said Harriet.

"I need you to meet with someone," said Waverly. Waverley was the head of MI6. Harriet knew that he and Tim had history and while they would work closely in the defence of the Realm, there was no love lost between them.

"I am in Cheltenham. I am not sure when I am back at Thames House." She was suspicious and intrigued that he had contacted her and not Tim.

"I know. There is a car downstairs."

Her first reaction was to refuse and phone Tim, despite the lateness of the hour. She voiced her thoughts.

"Please may we just keep this among ourselves for the moment? After you have heard what I have to say then, by all means, report all this back to Mr Burr. Deal?"

She was intrigued and her curiosity got the better of her. She dressed and ran a brush through her hair. She looked in the mirror. It would have to do. She had no intention of putting on her face for Waverley. She left the room and made her way along the corridor, down the steps into the lobby. It was empty. She opened the doors and walked outside. The car flashed its headlights. It was the standard issue Jaguar, beloved by the Government for its Britishness, despite that fact the Company was now owned by an Indian conglomerate.

The driver stepped from the car and opened the door. She sat in the back and they drove off. She knew that there was no point in engaging the chauffeur in conversation as there would be no disclosure of any worth from the man.

She realised that she was in for a bit of a journey as they were heading for Bristol. She looked at her watch. It was one twenty. She closed her eyes and decided a doze was in order. She was suddenly awakened from her dreams by a distant voice. "We are here," said

173

the driver as he leaned into the back of the car.

She stood up and stretched as she exited the rear of the Jaguar. She felt refreshed after her sleep in the back of the car. She looked round and realised that she was in Clifton, a well to do part of the City with a slight village feel to it. In the distance she could see the suspension bridge. Built by Isambard Kingdom Brunel, it was an iconic landmark of Bristol. .

"This way," she followed the driver down a flight of steps into the basement flat of the Victorian building. As she entered, the driver went to perform a pat down search.

"You can dispense with that," said Waverley as he entered the passageway from the door leading to the sitting room. He gestured for Harriet to follow him.

She entered the expensively furnished room. In the centre stood a tall individual, he was over the six foot two mark. Harriet was impressed with his look. His suit was tailored and good quality, shoes black and shiny and his rugged face had a serious but kind expression. Perhaps the night would be less of a chore than she had up to now expected it to be.

"Let me introduce Hunter Westbrook."

He offered his hand and she took it, His hand shake was firm but not crushingly so. He was confident and strong and she felt it as she looked into his grey, alert eyes. "Hi," he said. The illusion was shattered, another arrogant American that littered the intelligence World.

"Hunter has a story to tell," said Waverley as he offered Harriet a cup of coffee.

She sat on the red and gold sofa across the coffee table alongside Waverly as Hunter lowered himself into the leather buttoned captains chairs across from them. "As you have probably guessed, I am with the CIA. I am sorry to have this meeting so late. I have just flown into Heathrow, met with Bernard and we decided we needed to act tonight, before you went into GCHQ tomorrow and put the cat among the pigeons."

She looked at Waverley, "How did you know where I was?"

He looked slightly embarrassed. "You made no secret of your movements and we do have a few resources at MI6 specifically geared up to handle the odd bit of surveillance."

"Perhaps I should have asked why?"

"Ah! That is more to the point. After Mr Burr's address at the Joint Security meeting an idea came to me. As it turned out, both you and we were approaching the North Korean problem from different ends. You at MI5 had been tipped off by the Chinese and we had been approached by the CIA, who were as concerned as the Chinese were, that the US President was allowing the Koreans to get on with targeting an American warship in the East Sea," said Waverly.

"The President, a man as we know of somewhat unconventional opinions and a propensity for doing things his own way, decided to ignore Chinese overtures regarding Kim Jung –un's plans to attack US assets using our won military guidance systems. He has banned the CIA from furthering the matter. We could not act in contradiction to a direct Presidential Order, but the general feeling was that to allow the Koreans access to the US military GPS and allow them the possibility of sinking a US Navel Vessel was rash," said Westbrook.

"Not rash, fucking stupid," interrupted Waverley.

"I wouldn't use those words. I see the Presidential logic. Kim Jong-un blows up a US warship and China has no choice but to withdraw support for the regime in North Korea. The US is effectively in a state of war with North Korea and we bomb the bejesus out of the fuckers."

"Except, the North Koreans have a shit load of conventional

weapons pointed at South Korea and millions die, "said Harriet.

"It seems that the Presidential Logic does not extend that far into the future," said Westbrook.

"And we all know that the President has already accused the CIA of being his enemy and part of a conspiracy to undermine him," said Waverley.

"We know that the President does have a unique way of seeing and dealing with matters, but why am I here. More to the point why are you not talking to Tim?"

"Settle back and I shall begin," said Westbrook. "Many moons ago, when Elaine Wilkins, the previous boss of MI5 was with us, we had a joint arrangement. We, that is to say the CIA, was granted access to an MI5 asset, code named "Ding Dong". Ding Dong was a refugee from the North who fled to South Korea. He came to England with the help of MI5."

"Don't tell me, he was a plant, a spy for Kim Jong-un and Elaine turned him," said Harriet.

"Bernard was right about you. You are a very smart cookie. You are absolutely right but she did more. She ensured he worked in intelligence and got GCHQ to boost him through the ranks. Well at least on paper. MI5 fed bits of intelligence to North Korea, supposedly from Ding Dong. They had no idea that he was a double agent and came to trust their source".

"So what has it to do with me? Tim surely knows all this?"

"We sort of doubt that. You see Ding Dong died shortly after he was turned, nothing dramatic, a heart attack, Elaine decided to not acknowledge the fact and kept him going. In effect MI5 was Ding Dong."

"Right, so what's the problem?"

"Well, firstly, she was running him off the books, then as that became increasingly impractical, she handed him to the CIA. We have kept him going for twelve years now. Now we need to use him. We need to actually have him do something," said Westbrook.

"I repeat, what's the problem?"

"We need Ding Dong to insert a routine giving access to North Korea to the Command and Control structure of the British Armed Forces. Oh, and we need our deceased asset to do it in four days time to coincide with the joint US and South Korean navel exercises in the East Sea."

Harriet looked at Waverley who avoided her questioning gaze. "Ok, I see the problem in that Ding Dong is an ex Ding Dong and that it is fairly difficult to get dead people to do anything, but surely all you need to so is approach GCHQ or Tim, or both and put your plan to them?"

"It is not quite that simple, analyse the situation. The CIA has been ordered not to act by the President. The British, including Mr Burr, have no knowledge of Ding Dong. If the Director of the CIA approached MI5, Mr Burr would have to get approval from the Home Secretary. They would contact the US and the CIA would be exposed. It would not get off the ground."

"Why can't MI6 get involved, if it is such a good idea?" Harriet looked at Waverley for the answer.

"How, we would if we could. We can't gain accesses to GCHQ, but you are already here. You can."

"You want me to pretend to be Ding Dong, not tell Tim and hack into the Command and Control structure of the Nations defence system? And put in a bit of code dreamt up by the CIA?" said Harriet.

"Pretty much," said Westbrook.

"If you could see your way," said Waverley.

"How am I supposed to do it, even if I wanted to? I can't just sit around waiting at GCHQ looking at my watch can I?"

"I think you can. You go back to Thames House tomorrow and have a meeting with Tim and Madeleine. You tell them that you have identified a potential mole at GCHQ and that you suspect that they will act against the US fleet in four days time. They send you back to GCHQ to track and trap the imaginary Korean agent."

Harriet already had her list,. Kevin Drew, Shirley Worth and herself, that she would present the following morning at Thames House, before returning to GCHQ as the mole for the CIA and MI6 with Tim's blessing.

"What's in this bit of code you want me to insert?"

A big smile spread across her face as Westbrook told her. "Oh that is good, in fact it is fucking brilliant," she said." I'll do it."

Chapter 39

Following the intervention at the last moment by the Director of the CIA, the President, his cabinet and the Joint Chiefs of Staff took the advice and did "fuck all."

They watched as the North Korean missiles were launched. They flew into space heading for their target in Guam. "They are going to bomb our base," said the President. "I knew I should never have listened to you idiots at the CIA. Fake fucking news, that's all I get from all of you, fake news"

"Mr President just wait and see, please," said the Director.

"If you are wrong about this I shall be firing somebody," said the President.

"That will make a change," muttered one of the aids.

"Who said that?"

"Look Mr President, look at the screen."

Suddenly three of the missiles disappeared from the tracking. "What has happened?" asked the Commander in Chief of the USA.

"I think you will find that they have blown themselves up," said the Director.

"There is still one left heading for Guam."

"Or not, "replied the Director.

They watched as the missile changed course and headed for

Japan. "Now they are attacking the Japanese," said the President.

"Don't worry. We have warned their military to do nothing. They will, however, put on a big show of going on full alert and making protestations in the UN," said the Director.

There was silence as the missile flew over Japan. There was relief as it broke up and crashed harmlessly. "Show over," said the Director. "All that's left to do is get the World to condemn Kim Jung-un's provocative and flagrant breach of international law."

The Director of the CIA turned to Hunter Westbrook as the meeting broke. "Thank Waverley at MI6 for his help for me will you?"

"I think Harriet Shaw deserves the credit for this one, after what she has been through. Don't you?" said Westbrook.

***

Harriet sat in the semi darkness at Tim's bedside holding his hand. She did not want thanks, she wanted Tim. She squeezed his hand as the tears ran down her cheeks. "I love you," she whispered into the cold night.

Nicholas E Watkins

TANKER

Also by Nicholas E Watkins

Bank

Dealer

Oligarch

Steel

Hack

About the Author

Nicholas Watkins lives on the Coast with his wife and has four children He is a retired Accountant and has a Degree in Economics. He worked in the City of London for many years.

Hack

.

Chapter 1

The Hilux pulled up outside the laboratory and parked. The Moon sat low on the horizon and the first red glow of dawn lit up the dry desert sky. All was still, save for the barking of a dog. Security for this sector of the storage facility was in the hands of the Iraqis. Despite being the only thing moving at that time of the morning, the vehicle had not been challenged and no alarms were sounded as it drove into the inner compound.

On paper, the security around the complex of buildings forming the oil storage facility near Basra was impressive. ISIS had looked at it on many occasions as a potential target, but determined that the security presence was too high and their losses would be unacceptable. The laboratory, situated in its own area away from the main buildings, was, in contrast, perceived as far less of a target by the owners. They had neglected it in their assessment of threat levels, so security here was far less comprehensive.

The occupants of the truck sat waiting tensely in the darkness. They were armed with assault rifles, they would have no hesitation in using them if the need arose. They were committed to the aims of ISIS and would happily die as Martyrs in achieving them.

One of the truck's occupants was no more than a boy of sixteen, but he had the hatred of a thousand years in his heart. His Father and Uncles had all opposed the British occupation. It was part of his being, ingrained from childhood. He had seen how the invaders had gradually been defeated, driven back into their compound and finally isolated into a small, defensive position at the airport. He had helped fire the mortars into their base. He had seen their defeat and knew they were weak. He believed, in the end, ISIS would prevail and the Caliphate would be restored.

His companion was slighter in build but older, in his mid-thirties and with a pock marked face. He had been part of Saddam Hussein's army when the invasion had taken place. When the Coalition forces had overthrown the Dictator, they had disbanded the army. It had left him with a gun and no income. He had no love for Hussein and the then ruling Ba'th party but, he at least had an income and had been able to feed his family. It had not taken long for him to become disillusioned with the so called liberators of his Country and he now saw them as an occupying force.

"He should be here by now," said the older of the two. He looked at his watch. They had been there for nearly an hour. They waited another twenty minutes before the door to the laboratory opened and light spilled out across the compound. They jumped from the cab and, slinging their rifles over their shoulders, ran to the beckoning figure.

"Quiet, follow me," said the man in the lab coat. The technician moved swiftly down the corridors, turning left and right. He used his security pass to open doors and led them further into the building. He stopped and pointed to the radioactive symbol and the warning sign above the door. "My pass will take us no further," he said, leaving them outside the door and returning to his job in another part of the building.

The young boy sneaked a look through the glass panel at the top of the door. "Be careful and keep your head down. What did you see?" said his companion.

"Five of them, they are putting their coats on and getting ready to go home." They knew their shift was due to finish at six a.m. the intruders' information was proving to be correct. Unsupervised, they had developed the habit of knocking off early. They waited quietly until the door opened and the workers began to gather up their belongings. The first worker stepped through the door, bidding goodbye to his colleagues. The boy leapt to his feet and struck him in the face with the butt of his rifle, smashing teeth and breaking bone. The technician staggered backwards into his departing colleagues, his hands clutching his bleeding face. The older of the two pointed his rifle at the group, moving it from side to side. They stepped back, dropping their coats and bags to the floor.

"Put your fucking hands down. This isn't a cowboy movie," he said. "You know what we want, so let's not make this difficult for any of us, OK?"

The workers looked at each other, their team leader, an American, decided to speak, "How do you intend to transport it?"

"Just stick it in a box or bag."

"You will be exposed to a massive dose of radiation. More than an hour or two and you will get very ill and possibly die. Do you realise that? This material needs to be handled with extreme caution."

"Do we look like the kind of people who give a fuck? Now stop pissing about and bag it up for us, unless you'd like to die before it kills us." The head technician began the process of removing the radioactive rods from the calibrating machines and placing them in boxes. He and another technician then unlocked the radiation proof safe and removed the rest of the material, stored for intended future use and put it in the bag along with the rods.

"Give us your cell phones." The workers did as they were told, while the duo ripped the internal phones from the walls. "Now, we are trying to let you live, but we need to escape without you causing us a problem. We'll lock you in and smash the key pad on the other side. We know that will only keep you in here for a very short while, but think on this. If you raise the alarm, all of you will be dead by this time tomorrow and all your families will be dead by the time you get home. You are all Iraqis, apart from this man and you live here. We know you. We know your families. We know where you live and we will kill anyone who betrays us." He drew a small pistol and shot the American head of department in the face to underline the message. The rest of the group cowered and watched in shock as their boss fell to the floor. They had the message loud and clear.

The two men walked out to the truck, struggling under the weight of their radioactive load. "Why are you letting them live? They could raise the alarm?" said the boy.

"The tall ugly one is my cousin."

****

At the petrol station at Qa'im, just inside Iraq on the Syrian border, two ISIS fighters waited in a Ford Galaxy mini bus that was rapidly becoming hot and sticky inside. They had been there for some time, one of them got out and relieved himself. He returned to the bus, "Do you think they are coming? They are very late."

"We wait."

"We are very exposed here. The Security Forces could easily pick us up."

"We wait," said the other with finality.

So they waited and finally the convoy of heavy trucks came through the checkpoint at the border. They were escorted by guards travelling in lightly armoured vehicles. Scant attention was paid to the convoy and they were, more or less, just waved past by the Iraqis. The border was like a sieve and smugglers for the Government and the opposing factions traveled virtually unhindered between Iraq, Turkey and Syria. Trade between the three was probably more vigorous than before the conflict had started. The region had descended into total chaos. Fighters were going one way and insurgents the other, guns in, guns out, drugs and Jihadi brides were passing for good measure. The whole area was a complete security shambles.

The convoy pulled over to swap the escort for the next leg of the journey. The drivers got out of the assorted trucks and HGV's, relieved themselves, ate, faced towards Mecca and prayed. The occupants of the Galaxy joined them in prayers. By now a small fleet of trucks and cars had arrived in the area. It was apparent, that on crossing the border, the truck drivers all had small business ventures going with various locals smuggling items from one side of the border to the other. The gas station had descended into a mini bazaar.

It was a very simple matter for the mini bus occupants to help the driver of the truck carry the large box and place it in the rear of the Galaxy. "Sorry for the delay lads," said the driver "got held up on the road. It seems there was a change in the group that controlled a stretch of the highway. It took an age to sort out the bribe to allow us to pass. It cost me another eight hundred dollars to deliver your goods."

They knew that he was bumping the price up and they guessed he had probably paid a tenth of that. They were in no mood to haggle and gave him the extra. The driver was almost embarrassed by their lack of bargaining, but he, of course, accepted the extra cash.

The Ford Galaxy pulled away from the stop and headed south. If anyone had pointed a Geiger counter at it, they would have seen the needle go off the scale.

******

There were three bombings in Baghdad that day and over a hundred people were either dead or injured. The hospitals were struggling to cope with the injured and dying. ISIS was under pressure and they had been losing ground recently. They were stepping up their bombing campaign, part in retaliation, but also in order to let the World know they were still a force to be reckoned with.

189

The University was in a state of chaos. A targeted bomb had left the Campus in disarray. Students and staff were among the dead, dying and injured. Ambulances, security forces, police and militia were all engaged in the action. Chaos and panic had spread across the Campus.

The three ISIS members were looking for the Metallurgy Faculty and referring to a map of the building. Soon, they located the secure facility. Security today, however, was totally lacking following the carnage outside. The combination of suicide bombings and the random shooting into the crowd of students had made anyone, with the slightest instinct of self–preservation, get well clear of the Campus. They marched along the corridor to the store of radioactive material and literally, just blew the doors off with a small, plastic explosive charge. They walked back out with a holdall stuffed with the deadly radioactive material, got in a car and drove off. ISIS had just gone nuclear.

Chapter 2

The rain dripped through the hole in the sun awning into the bucket placed on the terrace by the bar owner. There was a large puddle where the bucket had over spilled. A young couple made a dash for the café, the male, wearing flips flops, slipped and nearly fell. The female was more sure footed and reached their table in a less dramatic fashion.

The tables and chairs on the terrace outside the Terminus Café, were a random collection of plastic, cane and metal. They had obviously been collected and replaced over the years and were a total mismatch. The Patron came out and, nearly slipping and falling himself, emptied the bucket that was filling at such a rapid rate in the downpour, served little purpose. Tim looked at the sagging awning, the red stripes faded into the greying white background and wondered, given that the rip in the awning was no bigger than six or seven centimetres, why the owner had not applied a piece of duct tape. Perhaps duct tape was rare in France, or perhaps the owners just could not be bothered and accepted the heyday of the Terminus Café, located directly opposite Menton railway station, had long since passed.

Tim sat with his back to the Café with the open glass door to his right giving him a clear view of the terrace, the station car park and the coming and goings of those entering and leaving the railway station entrance. He stirred his double espresso, three sugars, too many. He kept meaning to cut down, but somehow, forgot each time he put spoon to cup.

To his left there sat the cowboys. Two almost identically dressed men with white beards, stained orange with nicotine. They wore black leather sleeveless jerkins, white stained T shirts and black faded leather cowboy hats with large cross stitching on the brims and crowns. Their sleeping bags and Worldly possessions were stacked under cover in a shop doorway to the left of the Café. Their hands shook as they lifted their coffee to their lips, which the patron's wife had placed on the table in front of them a moment before. They were obviously regulars. The dog that emerged from the Café ran to greet them and was instantly scooped up onto one of their laps by trembling hands.

On Tim's right was a large red and white bag on a chair. Beside it, on the table, were three further, smaller plastic carrier bags stuffed with old clothes. The owner appeared from the Café and stood by the bags. She was in her fifties, hair long and dirty. Her hands also trembled as she struggled to raise a cup to her lips. The drug and alcohol abuse were etched in her face and thin body. She was dressed in flimsy, floral patterned beach trousers, a leopard blouse and a beige wrap around cardigan. Her feet were dirty, her toenails uncut and her toes forced over and under each other by the large bunions on the side of her, flip flop clad, feet. At some stage she must have had a life and obviously had loved her high heeled shoes. Tim imagined her as a young girl, dressed smartly, with her designer shoes and handbags, going to the Casino in Menton, or dancing in the night clubs. No longer desirable, broken and addicted, all her possessions in bags, she relied on the Terminus Café for her morning ablutions. She hopped nervously around the table, taking alternate sips of coffee and dragging on a roughly rolled cigarette that occasionally stuck to her lips.

Tim took another sip of his very sweet coffee and looked up to see a group of four men running from a black van to the cover of the terrace. There was more slipping and sliding on the treacherous wet tiles before they reached the safety of the chairs and sat at a table. The bucket was now overflowing, as the rain continued to pour

192

down. Thunder could be heard in the distance. The patron appeared with croissants and coffees and greeted the arrivals. Their jackets showed them to be railway workers. A fifth man dashed in and joined them and was greeted loudly by his co-workers.

So far, not one of the Café's customers fitted the bill of the man he was expecting to meet. He ordered another espresso and again put too much sugar in it. Tim, whose real name was Anthony Burr, had acquired the nick-name from his schoolmates. They had been unable to resist the opportunity for the joke, a "chip off the old block, timber," so the name stuck with him. He had been waiting at the Café for nearly an hour so far. Tim was forty one and looked out of place as he sat in the rain in the faded establishment. His clothes were a cut far above those of the other customers and his well-groomed appearance made him conspicuously noticeable. He felt uncomfortable.

This weekend had certainly not turned out as expected. He had anticipated spending a jolly few days at the Hotel Lewes in Monaco, watching the Grand Prix and perhaps getting a bit of sun. Today was race day and he had his place reserved on a nice yacht facing the track. Instead, he was sat, in probably the grubbiest café in the Cote D'Azure, doing someone else's job in the rain.

He had joined the civil service after he left Selwyn, Cambridge. He had done well enough, with a two one degree, to get a job in the Home Office. After a few years he was transferred to help out the long suffering Ambassador in Paris, where he would use his knowledge of foreign affairs to brief him daily with what was happening in the World. Technically, he was employed as an intelligence officer. Sounded like a spy but, in reality, he read the local papers, checked the briefings from the various government departments and made sure the Ambassador had a clear picture of the current situation and a clear understanding of what the current policy thinking was. After working in Thames House for a couple of years, he finally got Paris and was on this beano in Monaco. Along with the Ambassador, staff, some trade delegation chaps, he had managed to wangle the invite for himself to watch the Grand Prix, from a yacht booked by the Turkish trade delegation, in the Marina.

A note had been passed to the Ambassador's aide and as they had no one spare, here he was sat in the rain, waiting to meet a contact who, presumably, had a bit of inside information on trade or some such thing, while everyone else was tucking into a champagne breakfast on a luxury yacht.

He looked at his watch. His contact was late. The couple had left and the railway workers were making their way across the car park to the station. The itinerant cowboys appeared to be texting. How odd the World was. Nowhere to sleep, but you had a mobile phone. The table on the other side of the door was now occupied by a black man with a large suitcase on wheels, not his contact, a traveller perhaps? Not so, he clearly was the supply centre for the horde of beach hawkers that sold cheap goods on the beaches. He was approached by further Africans and goods were swapped around and money changed hands. The bag lady was looking at a mobile phone on offer from a beach trader, but there was still no sign of his contact.

The rain had stopped, the hills beyond were still bathed in a grey mist and rain and the distant sound of thunder could still be heard. He looked at his phone, checking the Grand Prix update. It was raining in Mote Carlo as well and the start of the race was under threat. He had now waited for nearly an hour and half. Enough he thought and made his way inside to settle up.

No one was to be seen, clearly service was not a priority at the Terminus Café. He heard voices from a side room. He stood and waited for a while. In the end, with no sign of anyone, he made his way towards the sound. He stood in the doorway. The family were sat around a table, covered with a red and white plastic check table cloth, having their breakfast. He stood. They looked quizzically at

194

him. "The bill," he said.

Reluctantly, the wife got to her feet and making him feel as though he was a nuisance by being a paying customer, she walked to the bar.. He followed her. His French was poor, GCSE standard. He could not understand the number being requested and pointed to the till which should have displayed the amount or printed off a bill but did neither. This caused a blast of French. The till was clearly not in the regular habit of being used. Cash in hand was the order of the day here. He removed ten euros and offered it to her. Success, change and he tipped her fifty cents. He had to admit, that although not salubrious, the Terminus Café was value for money.

He turned to leave, feeling that the morning had been a waste of time and effort. "Monsieur pour vous?" she handed him an envelope from behind the bar. It was addressed "L'homme Angletere," vague but effective.

Outside, he pulled out the note and read." Hotel Belgique, Room 15, Rue de la Gare. After 10, the concierge goes at 9. Code 8476, Stereogram." His heart sank. He would have to come back tonight. This was not the fun break he had hoped for.

He realised he was already in the Rue de la Gare. He glanced down the road and could clearly see the Hotel Belgique. He considered the note. "Who calls them self Stereogram?" he said to himself as he made his way across the car park to the railway station.

The rain had stopped in Menton, at least. He had purchased a return ticket in Monaco, so he went straight to the platform. The train was on time, but crowded with race goers. The journey took ten minutes with two stops. Then the problems began. He knew he needed to buy his ticket now for his trip back to Menton that evening. The queues would be huge after the race. Leaving the train, he tried to make his way to the main ticket concourse, but was blocked by a group of race officials. The crowds were being controlled by the seat numbers to their positions around the circuit. He tried to explain that he wished only to purchase a ticket, but that was clearly not in the remit of the marshals who ushered him off in the opposite direction. The station, he had to admit, was spectacular, clad in pink marble and spotlessly clean. Despite its architecture and splendour, he was losing interest in its elegance as he walked the whole underground route to end up at the other end of the town.

The streets were packed with race goers, street traders and race officials marshaling the pedestrians. Everywhere was jammed and everyone, it appeared, was going in the opposite direction to him. The rain had started again and was tipping down. He was very wet and fed up by the time he finally made it back to the station ticket office. He finally bought his return ticket to Menton. It was nearly two o'clock by the time he returned to the hotel to find everyone had left for the yacht. A pass to allow him access to the Marina had been left behind the desk, but he would have to get himself there. The Ambassador and the rest of the party had a nice escorted limo drive. He, on the other hand, would be back in the crowd, marshalled and wet. He set off with his recent purchase of a grey and white souvenir Monaco umbrella.

Chapter 3

Berat woke to the smell of tea, simit bread and the sound of hammering downstairs. His Mother was busy in the room next door, where she and his Father slept and where they all ate and watched television. Although it was just seven in the morning, he knew his Father had been up for hours working in the shop downstairs.

The whole flat smelt of leather, always of leather. They lived above his Father's cobblers shop. By the time he and his brothers were fed in the morning and went down the stairs to go to school, his Father would be busy at work. Piles of shoes were stacked up in the house, in the shop or outside waiting in pairs on the pavement, either for sale or collection. His Father was not the only cobbler in the street. The whole street up and down had the scene repeated. His trip anywhere, always started by passing between piles of footwear on the pavement surrounding his home in either direction.

His friends Emir and Ahmet were waiting to walk to school with him, He made his way past shoes and said goodbye to his Father who sat on the floor with a bradawl in his hand and a shoe on the last. His Father always said, "Work hard and get an education. You don't want to end up doing this all your life."

He took on board what his Father had said. So he had worked hard and had an education. Now a grown man, he sat on the wall overlooking the Bosphorus. The noise of the traffic on the road behind him was deafening. Vehicles of all shapes, sizes and ages streamed past, many blasting thick plumes of oil burning smoke. He suspected that Turkish emissions laws for vehicles, like many other laws, were not strictly enforced. In some ways the Country had come a long way since he was a child, in others it was going backwards. Ataturk, the Father of the modern Country, had created a secular government distinct from the religion. For a while, with the exception of the odd military coup, it had functioned, but now the State was more repressive and fundamentalism was on the rise.

Stretching in front of him was the sea, glistening with patches of oil and pollution. The oil tankers lined up to enter the Bosphorus, the twenty mile long north-south strait that joins the Sea of Marmara to the Black Sea and separates Europe and Asia. The ships were so large and appeared so close that you felt you could reach out and touch them. They seemed like toy boats in a bath. He had grown up with this sight all his life, but it still continued to captivate him. Now, in his mid-thirties, working as a civil servant, he longed for the simplicity in his life as it had been as a child, playing in the streets of Istanbul.

The Bosporus was just a part of his everyday life, from childhood he had taken it for granted. He remembered, as he gazed on the comings and goings of the vast ships, the day he had gone to University. His Father had gathered the whole family, brothers, cousins, aunts, uncles and friends to celebrate. His Father's pride was so great that he felt the burden to succeed weighing on him. He set himself to nothing but study and achievement. He did succeed, a first class degree followed by a masters and a well-paid secure job in government. He had taken extra language courses and spoke perfect French and English. He now travelled frequently around the World, acting as translator for the great and good in government and commerce. He knew that the English name Bosphorus came from the Greek bous, meaning cow and poros, meaning crossing, cow crossing. The legend went that Zeus had an affair with Io. When his wife Hera got wind of it she turned Io in a cow and created a horsefly to sting her bottom. It hurt so much that Io, the now cow, jumped across the strait.

He smiled to himself as he thought of cows jumping over the queue of tankers waiting to move oil around the Globe. His smile faded as he thought of Emir and Ahmet, brothers. He had grown up with them, shared school, fights, and sexual adventures. They were more like his own brothers or his family than friends. Their lives, of course, had diverged, he to University while they had remained in the grubby backstreets of Istanbul scraping a living as best they could. They were still close, but their life experiences were separated by a gulf wider than the Bosporus. He knew that, with their increasing frustrations and poverty, they had become more and more fundamentalist in their beliefs.

Behind him he could hear the call to prayers ringing out across the city. It was not that he was a bad Muslim, it was that he was more tolerant and inclined to live and let live. He valued peace. He had seen enough suffering acting as a translator around the Globe to know that the World did not need a helping hand down the road to more pain. Ahmet, the younger of the two brothers, had first become involved actively with the Fundamentalist Brotherhood when he was in his late teens. Like all young men, he had imagined himself the hero, fighting for truth and Allah, saving the poor, fighting the good fight. Berat reflected, as a child watching the old kids' television programs of jousting knights rescuing damsels, he had also seen its appeal. He knew all young boys yearned to be heroes and brave and the Muslim Brotherhood movement offered the chance to fight the corrupt and gain glory.

Ahmet started attending the more hard-core seminars held at the Mosques, meeting with other frustrated young men and searching the internet for like-minded individuals. It was not long before his brother Emir was being drawn into the more radical form of Islam as well. Now in their thirties, they wanted change. The idea of secular government was an insult to them, their beliefs and above all, to Allah. A trip to Syria had hardened their resolve and they were committed to the cause. Berat, to an extent, humoured them, not wishing to lose touch with that part of his life and his roots in the streets of Istanbul. He had been guilty, to an extent, of letting them think he was right there with them.

Celik, his wife was their younger sister. Berat had known her as the little pest that the three of them had teased as children. That had changed one summer when he came back from University. They fell in love and married. She was a good wife but shared many of her brothers' beliefs. Berat knew that, as her husband, she respected his wishes and never voiced her opinions to his more secular colleagues they mixed with.

As he sat watching the sun coming down and turning the sky bright red, yellow and lavender, it seemed to him that it was like an omen. His World was changing, he had not asked for it but it was. He now had choices, choices that Allah should ask no man to make.

Berat had been excited at being part of the delegation going to Monte Carlo. Of course, French was his specialist language and he would head the team of four translators working with him. It was a chance to influence the British. They all knew their support was key to Turkey's entry into the European Union. He knew that every opportunity would be taken to polish their record on human rights, their commitment to fighting terrorism and to demonstrate their commitment to the West.

He was finalising the details with his team when Yosuf had asked him to step into his office. Berat immediately sensed that this was not the usual, checking on final details, type of meeting.

"Take a seat," Yosuf commanded. This was unusual, Yosuf was not a command type of person. Berat feared he had made an error and was to be hauled over the coals. "There is a problem, a big problem," Berat feared that his job was on the line as Yosuf continued.

"You are married to Celik and she has two brothers, does she not, Emir and Ahmet?" he did not pause for a reply." "As I said, there is a problem." He seemed to struggle to find the words to continue. The word problem hung in the air. He took a deep breath. "They are to be arrested."

Berat's mouth hung open in surprise, "Arrested, for what."

"Security matters"

"My wife?"

"She will be fine, do not worry on that account; I have vouched for you both. I told them I know you to be a loyal servant of the State and totally dependable."

At that moment Berat realised his suspicions of Yosuf were well founded. He had always suspected that there was far more to Yosuf's role than just head of the Foreign Office translation department. He now realised, in that role, Yosuf could travel around and liaise with his Country's espionage resources globally. He had worked with him for nearly seven years and this confirmed that he was definitely part of Counter Intelligence. With hindsight, Berat began to see historic events in a new light, burglaries, disappearances and killings fell into focus. He was not just a translator. He was part of the cover for the State to carry out what it needed to do.

"You realise you must not warn them, nor tell your wife, don't you?"

Berat nodded, but he knew that he would and that decision would change his life for ever.

22408922R00120

Printed in Poland
by Amazon Fulfillment
Poland Sp. z o.o., Wrocław